"Dance with me."

It was pure charm—the rough baritone voice, the slightly lopsided smile, the touch of that single finger against her lips. And its simplicity caught her off guard. So did the unexpected stab of desire she felt to do exactly as he asked.

Disconcerted, Edie shook her head. "No," she said. "Thank you."

"Why not?" His fingers lightly pressed her wrist. His eyes wouldn't let hers go.

"You're not supposed to ask why not," she said. "It's bad manners."

A corner of his mouth quirked. "I thought it was bad manners for you to say no."

She felt like a gauche teenager, her cheeks burning. But she managed a little shake of her head. "I'm sorry. I can't."

"Can't?" He cocked his head. "Or won't?"

RITA® Award-winner **ANNE MCALLISTER** was born in California, spent formative summer vacations on the beach near her home and on her grandparents' small ranch in Colorado and visiting relatives in Montana. Studying the cowboys, the surfers and the beach volleyball players, she spent long hours developing her concept of "the perfect hero." (Have you noticed a lack of hard-driving, Type-A businessmen among them? Well, she promises to do one soon, just for a change!)

One thing she did do, early on, was develop a weakness for lean, dark-haired, handsome lone-wolf type guys. When she finally found one, he was in the university library where she was working. She knew a good man when she saw one. They've now been sharing "happily ever afters" for over thirty years. They have four grown children and a steadily increasing number of grandchildren. They also have three dogs who keep her fit by taking her on long walks every day.

Quite a few years ago they moved to the Midwest, but they spend more and more time in Montana. And as Anne says, she lives there in her head most of the time anyway. She wishes a small town like her very own Elmer, Montana, existed. She'd move there in a minute. But she loves visiting big cities as well, and New York has always been her favorite.

Books by Anne McAllister

Harlequin Presents®.
#2944—*The Virgin's Proposition*
#2871—*One-Night Mistress...Convenient Wife*

All backlist available in ebook.

THE NIGHT THAT CHANGED EVERYTHING
ANNE MCALLISTER

~ Tall, Dark and Dangerously Sexy ~

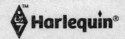

TORONTO NEW YORK LONDON
AMSTERDAM PARIS SYDNEY HAMBURG
STOCKHOLM ATHENS TOKYO MILAN MADRID
PRAGUE WARSAW BUDAPEST AUCKLAND

Recycling programs
for this product may
not exist in your area.

ISBN-13: 978-0-373-52837-0

THE NIGHT THAT CHANGED EVERYTHING

First North American Publication 2011

THE NIGHT THAT
CHANGED EVERYTHING

For Peter, always.
And this time, especially, for Steve, with
thanks for the road trip and the memories.

CHAPTER ONE

HE WAS Trouble. With a capital *T*.

From the look of him, Edie thought as she watched Mr. Tall, Dark and Drop-Dead Gorgeous flash his brilliant smile at her starlet sister, Rhiannon, the whole *word* should be capitalized.

TROUBLE.

The precise sort of trouble she knew it was her job to prevent.

So Edie hovered beside a pillar in the Mont Chamion state ballroom assessing the situation as the wedding reception of her royal highness Princess Adriana and her handsome groom, well-known actor-director Demetrios Savas went on around her.

The orchestra was playing and couples all around her were dancing. It would have been better—*safer*—if Rhiannon had been dancing, too. Instead she was standing still, her body nearly pressed into that of the man she was talking to.

Was it too much to hope that Mr. Trouble would simply smile at her simpering, eyelash batting sister, set her aside and move away into the throng? He was clearly out of Rhiannon's league. Her sister might be beautiful and flirtatious, but this man looked to be in his mid-thirties, worldly, sophisticated and clearly had far too much of the "male animal" for Rhiannon who was barely twenty.

And not a very mature twenty, at that.

Edie watched as her sister put her hand on his arm and stood staring up at him with rapt fascination. Edie recognized the look. It could mean she was actually interested in what he was saying to her. Or it could mean that Ree was doing what she did best—acting. In either case, unless Edie intervened it would cause no end of trouble.

Edie willed Mr. Trouble to turn away, to find another admirer. Dancing couples obscured her view for a moment. But when she caught sight of them again, she could see he hadn't moved an inch. His expression was bemused as he smiled down at her sister. It gave him an enticing groove in one cheek. Rhiannon reached up a finger and stroked it.

Edie stifled a groan.

An elbow suddenly collided with her back. She turned, expecting an apology. Instead she found her mother glaring at her.

"Do something!" Mona Tremayne hissed. She gave Edie a speaking look, then smoothly turned back to Danish producer, Rollo Mikkelsen, slid her arm through his and blinded him with one of her patent Mona Tremayne Sex Goddess For The Ages smiles.

All Edie could think was, "Thank God Rhiannon hadn't perfected that bit of their mother's repertoire yet." But she seemed to be doing well enough on her own. Behind her as the music ended Edie detected what she thought was her sister's lilting giggle. It was joined by a deep baritone laugh.

Mona obviously heard it, too. She turned back from Rollo Mikkelsen and glowered, first at Edie, then over Edie's shoulder to where Rhiannon was about to make a big mistake.

So there was no help for it. Edie set her teeth grimly and turned away from her mother, knowing her duty. "Right. On my way."

As her mother's and sister's business manager, Edie's job was to keep their careers on track. She dealt with the finances, the business appointments, the offers, the contracts and the myriad demands that the world made on one of America's leading screen actresses and her up-and-coming starlet daughter.

All that was a piece of cake.

It was the hands-on meddling that Edie hated. She didn't

have to do it for her mother. Over the years Mona had certainly learned to take care of herself. And if she made mistakes, she had the clout to make them go away.

Rhiannon was another story.

Rhiannon was young and vulnerable, emotional and flighty. She was also genuinely kind and loving. It was a scary combination. Making sure Rhiannon had lots of projects to keep her focused was the best way to be sure she didn't sabotage herself, her life or her career.

Ordinarily Edie could manage that by keeping her sister's calendar booked, and she never had to leave California to do it.

But Mona had rung two days ago from Mont Chamion and said, "Pack your bags."

When her mother spoke in that brisk no-nonsense tone, Edie knew not to argue. Where Rhiannon was concerned, Mona's instincts were almost always spot on. If she foresaw trouble, it was better to tackle it head-on than to hope it might not happen. So Edie had dutifully flown halfway around the world ready to put out whatever potential fire might erupt.

But she hadn't expected to attend the wedding.

"Why ever not?" Mona had demanded. "Of course you're coming to the wedding. And the reception," she'd added firmly. "God only knows what mischief Rhiannon can get up to there— especially now that Very Nice Andrew is gone."

Very Nice Andrew—*long-suffering* Andrew was how Edie thought of him—was Rhiannon's fiancé. Her first love, he was absolutely right for Rhiannon, and they both seemed to know it—most of the time. When he and Rhiannon were together and blissful, Edie's life was relatively blissful, too.

But a lovers' quarrel had sent Andrew stalking out yesterday. And Mona was right, disaster could easily ensue if Rhiannon was left feeling unappreciated and unloved.

But still Edie had protested that she wasn't attending the wedding.

"Of course you are," Mona had said firmly that afternoon as

she'd slipped into the gown she was wearing for the wedding and motioned for Edie to lace the back panel. It was a simple sheath, royal blue, setting off Mona's amazing eyes, with an open V at the back which, as Edie laced it, offered a glimpse of Mona's still-creamy flesh. It was quietly sexy and titillating, showing just enough to remind the world that, at fifty, Mona Tremayne was still a very appealing woman.

"I'm not invited." Edie pulled the laces together. "And I'm not crashing a royal wedding."

Mona's gaze met hers in the mirror. "Nonsense. You're not crashing. You're my guest."

"Oliver is your guest."

Sir Oliver Choate, English actor and Mona's most recent co-star, had flown in from Spain yesterday afternoon expressly to escort Mona to the wedding.

"Besides Oliver," Mona said impatiently. "You need to be there. And you might meet someone…" Her voice trailed off, but she looked at Edie hopefully.

Edie's teeth set. Exactly what she'd been afraid of. Mona—matchmaking. She gave a long-suffering sigh of her own. "I'm not interested in meeting anyone, Mother."

"Don't call me Mother in public," Mora admonished. "You're nearly thirty, for goodness' sake!"

Edie laughed and shook her head, then gave an extra tug to the laces, making her mother suck in a sharp breath. "We're not in public, and I don't think they have the bedrooms bugged. Besides, you don't get parts for ingenues anymore. People know how old you are."

Mona sighed, then stood up a bit straighter. "I try not to think about it. Anyway—" she shoved a hand into her artfully wind-blown auburn hair "—you must come—even if you don't meet a soul," she added piously. Then she spoiled it by saying, "But honestly, Edie, you need to get back on the horse."

Start dating again, she meant. Get a life again. Get over Ben. But Edie didn't want to get over him. Why should she? Her husband, Ben, had been the best thing that had ever happened to her. And yes, he had been dead two and half years. But so what?

"I did," Mona pointed out, not for the first time.

"And how did that work out for you?" Edie said dryly.

Edie's father, Joe, had been killed in a horse riding accident when Edie was five. He'd been the love of Mona's life, and she'd spent the next twenty years trying to replace him with a succession of men who'd become Edie's stepfathers.

"I have wonderful children," Mona said, defiantly meeting her daughter's eyes in the mirror.

That was certainly true. Edie couldn't complain about her younger brothers and sisters. In fact Rhiannon, Grace, Ruud and Dirk were the best part of her life, the family that had become for her the one she and Ben had never had.

"You do," Edie agreed solemnly. She might not have shared her mother's determination where men were concerned, but she loved her siblings dearly.

"And one of them needs you," Mona had said, playing the trump card. "Tonight. Lord knows what will happen if Very Nice Andrew breaks off the engagement."

"Do you think he might?" Edie thought Andrew was besotted with her sister, but she supposed even he could be pushed too far.

Andrew Chalmers was twenty-three, a three-event Olympic swimming medalist, cute as a button and an all-around nice guy, to boot. He had been head over heels in love with Rhiannon since they were in high school together, poor fool.

Though, to be fair, when she wasn't flirting outrageously with everything in trousers just because she could, Ree genuinely seemed to be in love with Andrew, too. He steadied her, brought out the caring, sweet side of her. And both Mona and Edie were delighted.

A month ago, Andrew had asked her to marry him. Instantly Rhiannon had said yes. They were getting married next summer.

Rhiannon was happily planning their wedding. Or had been—until yesterday's quarrel.

It hadn't been subtle. Right there in the middle of one of the Mont Chamion's most elegant royal reception rooms in front of the king and most of the royal family, Rhiannon had pitched a fit when Andrew had said he was leaving to go to a swimming competition in Vancouver.

"But what about me?" Rhiannon had wailed. "You're taking me to the wedding!"

"I'm not, actually," Andrew had said in calm, reasonable tones. "And you knew that, Ree. I said so last week when you wanted me to come over. I said I could come but I had to leave on Friday."

"But I want you to be with me!"

"You can come with me. I said so," he reminded her.

But Rhiannon hadn't wanted to miss the royal wedding. And she'd been sure she could twist Andrew around her finger once she got him here. But Andrew had more backbone than that. And no flood of tears or flurry of words had deterred him. He had stalwartly held his ground and soon thereafter caught a flight to Paris and then to Vancouver. Privately Edie had cheered him on, glad he wasn't knuckling under to every demand Rhiannon made.

But she had worried, too, because Rhiannon had been in High Drama Mode ever since.

"She'll 'do something,'" Mona predicted. "I know it. And so do you. She'll ruin it, shoot herself in the foot."

Shooting herself in the foot, literally, was not Rhiannon's problem. Doing something outrageous with an entirely inappropriate man just to spite Andrew was.

Rhiannon was one of the most beautiful young women Hollywood had ever seen. She was Marilyn Monroe at twenty. Betty Boop in the flesh. And she could flirt for England. Or Wales in this case as Rhiannon's father was the fiery Welsh poet,

Huw Evans. Rhiannon had dual-citizenship. And the ability to get into trouble no matter which continent she was on.

So here Edie was, lurking on the edges of the ballroom, clad in her sister's sparkly mauve dress that looked magnificent with Rhiannon's sun-kissed platinum-blonde tresses and deep golden tan, but made Edie's brown hair look dull and which washed out her fair skin, making her freckles stand out like spots. Even worse was the fact that Rhiannon's size seven matching heels were pinching Edie's size nine feet. It was like being stuck in a badly adapted version of Cinderella—and there wasn't a fairy godmother in sight. Of course there was no prince, either.

Only Mr. Trouble.

Even as Edie watched, Rhiannon cozied up to him, leaning closer, slipping her arm through his. Then she ran the fingers of her other hand down the front of his dinner jacket and giggled a breathless giggle at something he said. She tossed her head, making her hair dance in the light reflected from the crystal chandeliers. At the same time she tucked herself against him and reached up to playfully tousle his hair.

Edie swallowed a groan. Next thing you knew she'd start fiddling with his tie. *Undressing him!* Mona was right. Disaster was imminent.

Gritting her teeth against the blisters forming on her heels and toes, Edie pushed away from the pillar and made her way toward her sister.

"Ah, there you are!" she said cheerfully. She even managed to beam brightly though it felt more like a wince.

Rhiannon turned and tossed her hair again, obviously annoyed at having her flirtation interrupted. She was no fool. She had to know exactly why Edie was here. "What do you want?" Ree demanded.

Her tone had Mr. Trouble's dark eyebrows arching as he looked down his blade-straight nose at Edie, wordlessly asking the same question.

She flashed him a smile of polite acknowledgment, but focused on her sister. "I've had a text from Andrew." Which, fortunately, was absolutely true.

Rhiannon lit up, then remembered she was mad at Andrew and frowned. "Why's he texting you?" Her tone was accusatory.

"Can't imagine." Edie shrugged. "Maybe because you turned your phone off?"

Rhiannon's lower lip jutted out petulantly. "I didn't want to talk to him."

"Well, he wants to talk to you. Badly. He sounded desperate."

That might have been embroidering things a bit. The text had said, *Tell ur sister 2 turn her fone on. Need 2 talk.*

But he'd said "need." Didn't that mean "desperate"? Of course it did.

"Badly," Edie reiterated, to reinforce the point. Then she turned her gaze on the man still standing with his arm around Rhiannon. "Andrew is her fiancé," she said pointedly.

He let her go. Quite casually but deliberately, he eased his arm from beneath her hand and moved a step away. He looked at Rhiannon. "A fiancé?"

Ree lifted her shoulders in a sulky shrug. "He's not here," she said. But then she had the grace to appear a bit shamefaced. "We quarreled. He's not always right," she muttered.

Mr. Trouble didn't say anything, and Edie felt obliged to jump in and steer the situation. "Of course he's not," she said stoutly. "And now he's had plenty of time to think about things all the way to Vancouver. I'm sure he didn't mean to hurt you, Ree. He's probably missing you dreadfully."

"Do you think?" Suddenly Ree's tone was bright.

Edie nodded emphatically. "Call him."

But Rhiannon hesitated. She looked at the handsome man beside her, then her gaze measured the whole ballroom as if she were trying to decide what she'd be missing if she left: champagne, music, happy couples dancing past. Mr. Trouble who was, even in Edie's disapproving estimation, the handsomest man in the room.

Rhiannon looked disgruntled. "He should have stayed. *We* could have danced."

"Yes, but he wanted you to go with him, too," Edie reminded her. "It's a two-way street. He has a competition."

"But I'd have missed the wedding."

"And now you're missing Andrew."

Edie let that sink in for a few moments. Then she added almost offhandedly, "If you call him, you can tell him what Sir Oliver said about using his Scottish castle for your honeymoon."

It was the ultimate temptation. Ever since their engagement, Rhiannon's life had revolved around their wedding plans, and every detail had to be shared with Andrew. Sir Oliver's offer of his family's castle had been all Rhiannon could talk about last night—when she wasn't talking about how she was fed up with Andrew.

"Oh, all right." Rhiannon tumbled to the temptation exactly as Edie had dared hope. "I'll call him. I guess I should since he tried to call…and if he texted you…"

Ree sighed, then lifted her gaze to look at Mr. Trouble. "He loves me," she explained. "And I love him—even if he's maddening. So I probably should call him. But," she added a bit wistfully, "I really would have loved to see the architectural renovations in your bedroom."

"And I'd have been pleased to show them to you," he said gallantly.

Edie's jaw dropped. She slammed it shut at once. Rhiannon didn't notice. She gave them both a little wave and tripped gaily off toward the doors to the Great Hall where, please God, she would call Andrew and make up with him.

Edie watched her go, holding her breath until Rhiannon was out of sight. Then she turned to make her excuses and disappear, only to discover that the man Rhiannon had been pawing wasn't looking in the direction Rhiannon had gone.

His dark eyes were now on her. A slow smile touched his lips. And then he winked at her.

Winked!

Something kicked over in her chest. It was almost electric, as if she'd been dead and was suddenly jerked back to life.

Like Sleeping Beauty and the prince? she sneered at herself. But the sensation was so real and caught her so totally unaware that for a moment she couldn't speak. She hadn't felt this sort of awareness since Ben.

When she did finally find her voice, she said, "Architectural renovations in your bedroom?"

Next thing you knew he'd say he'd been going to show Rhiannon his etchings.

But Mr. Trouble just grinned at her and she felt another jolt. "Scout's honor," he said, eyes alight with amusement.

Edie refused to think it was funny. She glowered at him.

"You don't believe me? I'll show them to you." He offered her his arm.

Instantly Edie folded hers across her chest. "Don't be ridiculous! I'm not going to your room. And Rhiannon wouldn't have, either," she lied a second later, needing for some reason she didn't quite understand to deflect the focus back to her sister. "She does love Andrew. They just had a disagreement. And she...lost her head." Not to mention her sense of propriety. "She wasn't offering," she added firmly.

"No?" His brow lifted. "Apparently you didn't hear as much of the conversation as I did."

Edie's cheeks burned. "She wouldn't have—have..."

"Slept with me?" He was laughing at her now. "You don't think so?"

"No!" At least Edie hoped not.

"Well, don't worry, I wouldn't have slept with her."

Edie's eyes widened, and she was surprised again by another unexpected feeling, this time one of something akin to relief. "You...wouldn't?"

He shook his head, meeting her gaze. "Not on your life. She's a child."

"She's twenty."

He nodded. "Like I said, not my type."

"You have a type." It wasn't a question.

Of course he had a type. Men like him always did.

"Well, um, good," Edie said, because she felt obliged to say something in the face of the steady assessing look he was giving her. She started to back away.

He followed. "Who are you?" he demanded. His gaze was intent now, his eyes so dark they were almost black.

"Rhiannon's sister." No one ever believed it until Mona swore on a stack of Bibles that she'd given birth to them both. Her sister was blonde and busty, all curves and come-on. Edie was all angles, elbows and knees. Always had been. With nondescript brown hair and green eyes. Not the color of jade. Not the color of emeralds. Pretty much the color of grass. "Half sister," she corrected.

"Do you have a name, half sister?"

"Edie Daley."

Something else she and Rhiannon didn't have in common. Her sister was named after some ethereal mythological Welsh goddess. Edie was named after her father's mother.

"Ah. Edie." He grinned and reached out and tugged one of her nondescript locks of hair. "My grandmother's name."

Exactly.

"I'm Nick."

As in "up to the old nick," no doubt—as *her* grandmother used to say when describing the family's mischief makers.

"Nick Savas."

"Demetrios's brother?" Edie knew he had several, but she hadn't been introduced to any of them. She just knew that almost all of the tall dark-haired, sinfully gorgeous men at the wedding were related to the groom.

Nick shook his head. "Cousin."

Trust Rhiannon to flirt with a member of the groom's family. The most handsome member of the groom's family, come to that. All the Savas men were handsome as sin. But this one was definitely the most gorgeous of the lot.

That was doubtless why she'd felt the sudden jolt of awareness. She wasn't interested, but she wasn't dead! She was just able to appreciate a handsome man.

"I apologize if my sister's behavior was inappropriate, Mr. Savas—" she said politely, again beginning to edge away.

"Nick," he corrected.

She didn't repeat his name. She recognized it for what it was: an invitation to continue the conversation. And she didn't want to do that. Her awareness of him made her nervous, though she wasn't sure why.

"If you'll excuse me…" She turned abruptly to take the same route her sister had toward the doors. Her duty was done, she could go back to her room, shed the ugly dress, kick off the pinching shoes and spend the rest of the night with a good book.

But before Edie could take a step, strong fingers manacled her wrist, anchoring her right where she was. She looked back at him, eyes wide. "What?"

"You're not going to follow her and make sure she calls him, are you?"

"Of course not."

"So, why are you running off? Stay and talk to me." There was a smooth, persuasive note in his voice.

"I—" She stopped, wanting to say no, expecting herself to say no. She always said no. But now she couldn't seem to form the word. "About what?" she said finally, warily.

He raised a brow. "The architectural renovations in my bedroom?"

She couldn't help it. She laughed.

It was the sort of wry remark that Ben would have made. Her husband had never taken himself very seriously. And after years spent in her mother's world of overinflated egos, Ben's easy-going approach to life had been one of the things she'd loved the most about him.

She hadn't expected that same dry humor from Mr. Trouble, though. But Nick Savas laughed, too, then grinned at her. "There," he said. "See? I knew I could get you to smile."

Edie resisted the pull of attraction. "I've already smiled. I smile a lot," she contradicted him.

"But how often do you mean it?" he challenged softly.

"Often!"

"But not to me," he said. "Not until now."

She opened her mouth to protest, but he touched a finger to her lips to forestall her.

"Dance with me."

It was pure charm—the rough baritone voice, the slightly lopsided smile, the touch of that single finger against her lips. And its simplicity caught her off guard. So did the unexpected stab of desire she felt to do exactly that.

Disconcerted, Edie shook her head. "No," she said. "Thank you."

"Why not?" His fingers lightly pressed her wrist. His eyes wouldn't let hers go.

"You're not supposed to ask 'why not,'" she said irritably. "It's bad manners."

A corner of his mouth quirked. "I thought it was bad manners for you to say no."

She felt like a gauche teenager, her cheeks burning. But she managed a little shake of her head. "I'm sorry. I can't."

"Can't?" He cocked his head. "Or won't?"

Edie took refuge in the truth. She lifted her shoulders and said simply, "My feet hurt."

Nick did a double-take. Then he glanced down at the mauve leather pointy-toed high heels trapping her feet.

"Dear God." He scowled fiercely at them, then looked up to flash her a quick grin. "Come here." And he tugged her inexorably to one of the tables at the edge of the dance floor. "Sit."

It sounded more like a command than an invitation. But getting off her feet was a welcome prospect, so obediently Edie sat.

She expected he would sit down beside her or, even better and probably more likely, leave her there and go find some other woman to dance with. Instead he crouched down in front of her and, before she knew it, he'd taken both her shoes off and tossed them under the table.

She let out a little yelp. "What are you—?"

"I don't know why you women wear such terrible shoes." Nick shook his head, his dark eyes locking with hers accusingly, his fingers caressing her instep.

She started to say they were Rhiannon's, but his touch was robbing her of intelligible speech. And when he began to rub each of her pinched feet gently between his hands, she nearly moaned. It felt heavenly. And intimate. His touch sent bolts of awareness straight through her. She wanted him to stop—and at the same time nearly sobbed when he let go and pulled his hands away.

"There now." He stood up in one fluid movement. "Better?"

Edie looked up, dazed to see him looking down—imperious, in command, his gaze compelling.

All she could do was nod.

"Then dance with me." And he pulled her to her feet and straight into his arms.

It was magic.

He swirled her off her stocking-clad feet and led her into the waltz. She should have stumbled. She always stumbled when she danced.

Even when she'd danced with Ben at their wedding she'd felt self-conscious, always aware that Mrs. Achenbach, her cotillion instructor, had lamented that her clumsy pupil had two left feet. The words had taken up residence in her brain from the time Edie was ten years old. She absolutely believed them.

But tonight she had one of each—stocking-clad though they

were—and miraculously they did exactly what they were supposed to do: followed his.

Of course they did.

Because that was the sort of man he was. Nick Savas said, "Dance," and they didn't dare do anything else. Edie peeked down at her toes, amazed.

"Something wrong?"

Everything. Nothing. Edie shook her head, still dazed. It was like having an out-of-body experience. Or maybe like having an *"in-someone-else's-body"* experience. Like Cinderella's.

Certainly not her own.

She wasn't even supposed to be here. Didn't *want* to be here. Had no business being here—except for Rhiannon. And Rhiannon had already gone.

Instinctively Edie glanced around, looking for a clock. How close to midnight was it?

No way to tell. And Nick wasn't giving her a chance to look. They swirled and dipped and glided. Her liberated toes tingled and she would have wriggled them if she'd been able to do that and dance at the same time. It was the least likely thing she could imagine doing. She half expected someone to tap her on her shoulder and point out her lack of shoes, Or, worse, make a general public announcement.

But of course no one was looking at her. Especially not at her feet.

He had danced her all the way across the ballroom by this time. It was lovely, exhilarating. And yet she could only wonder how in heaven's name she was going to get Rhiannon's shoes back. She glanced around and couldn't even pick out where they'd left them.

"Now what?" Nick said gruffly.

"My shoes—"

"Not yours," Nick said with certainty.

"Well, no," Edie admitted. "Rhiannon's. But I can't just leave them there."

"We'll get them later." He dismissed the whole problem, but then he wasn't dancing at the royal wedding in his socks. "Smile," he commanded her. "I like it when you smile." And he smiled again, too, as if forming a smile of his own could prompt her.

It seemed that it could. Edie's lips curved. Apparently her mouth was as malleable as her feet.

Nick nodded. "Yes. Like that."

No wonder her sister had been pawing his dinner jacket.

Edie faltered at the thought. But the second her feet began to stumble, Nick caught her, drew her up again, pulled her close. Now her breasts pressed against his jacket. And as she was not overly well-endowed that meant all the rest of her was very close to him, too. Through the silk of her dress Edie could feel his legs brush against hers. If she turned her head, she could count individual whiskers on his jawline. And whenever she drew a breath, she smelled soap and a hint of woodsy aftershave.

Her knees wobbled. Nick held her closer still.

"I'm not a very good dancer," she apologized, trying to straighten and pull back.

But Nick didn't let go. "I'm enjoying it. Best part of the evening so far." His voice was a purr in her ear. The vibration sent a tingle all the way down her spine. And her brain leaped ahead, going exactly where she didn't want it to go.

So far?

How far was he expecting it to go?

"Now what?" he murmured as he must have felt her stiffen in his arms.

Edie gave a little shake of her head. "Nothing. I…I'm fine. I just thought of something."

"You need to stop thinking." She could hear the smile in his voice and as he turned his head, she thought she felt his lips against her hair. The shiver was back, sliding down her spine.

What on earth was wrong with her?

She hadn't felt like this in years. Hadn't felt the least flicker of interest in a man since Ben.

Her mother's insistence that she "get back on the horse" had fallen on deaf ears because she didn't feel any need to. And she refused to force things. But this wasn't forced. It was entirely involuntary—and very very compelling as Nick steered her closer to the orchestra. The music enveloped her, wrapping her in a ridiculous Cinderella fantasy.

Danger! her sensible self whispered.

But her dancing self, her wiggling-toes self, countered just as quickly: as long as she knew it was a fantasy, where was the harm?

It wasn't as if she believed in fairy-tale endings.

She'd learned at eighteen when heartthrob actor, Kyle Robbins, had broken her heart that fairy tales were fantasies, that real life romances didn't end in happily ever after. And if she'd dared to think that her marriage to Ben disproved that, well, she had only to remember the devastation of losing him.

So, she knew you couldn't count on happily ever after. She was immune.

So go ahead, she told herself. *Take it for what it is—a few minutes of enjoyment. It won't last, but who cares? It's one dance, one night. Nothing more.*

For the first time tonight her brain and her feet were in agreement. She smiled up at Nick Savas, wiggled her toes and gave herself over to the dance.

Nick Savas didn't do weddings.

Hadn't in years.

He hadn't wanted to come to this one, either. But when you were the cousin of the groom, on the one hand, and were currently restoring a wing of the bride's family's castle, on the other, you knew you didn't have a choice.

There was no way he could have continued working right through the royal wedding day—even though he would have preferred it. He didn't want to watch another happy couple make vows to each other for the rest of their lives. He didn't want to see the way they looked at each other with hope in their eyes and dreams in their hearts. Maybe it was selfish—all right, it damned well was selfish—but he didn't want to witness other people getting what he'd been denied.

Ever since his fiancée, Amy, had died two days before their own wedding, he'd turned his back on all that.

Savas weddings were particularly to be avoided not just because he would have to watch another of his cousins plight their troth, but because every single relative there seemed to consider it their responsibility to point out eligible women for him to meet. To marry.

Nick had no interest in marrying anyone.

No one seemed to get that. So ordinarily he took care to be on a different continent. But working on Mont Chamion's castle, meant he was here today. He'd had no choice.

"It will be lovely," his aunt Malena had assured him yesterday afternoon. "I think Gloria is bringing two of Philip's assistants. They're both young and unmarried," she added brightly, confirming his worst fears.

"Oh, yes," his aunt Ophelia gushed. "There will be lots of absolutely gorgeous women. You can take your pick."

But Nick didn't want his pick. So he'd arrived at the last minute, then sat in the back, avoiding the myriad Savas aunts, uncles and cousins, who, seeing him in attendance, would put one and one together. It was what they did. They couldn't help it. They had an ark mentality—the world was best arranged by twos.

Nick didn't dispute that. Hell, he absolutely believed it.

But there was no "best" for him anymore. Never would be.

When he heard the priest intone, "Do you take this woman…" his throat had tightened.

He shut his mind off, determinedly focusing instead on the various cherubim and seraphim floating above the congregation, studying them as if he were going to be tested on them which, once up on a time he had been, in a course on period architectural detail.

These were mid-seventeenth century from the look of them. Very baroque. Bernini would have been right at home.

"I now pronounce you man and wife."

Nick breathed a sigh of relief.

He would have escaped then, except his uncle Orestes had latched on to him before he could, determined to talk to him to see if he wouldn't like to come and restore the moldering gazebo on his Connecticut property.

At least it hadn't been an offer to introduce him to the new office girl. Silently Nick had counted his blessings as he went along the receiving line, congratulated his cousin, Demetrios, and kissed the glowing bride.

After the dinner, which he had contrived to eat in the company of his uncle Philip's triplet daughters because no one could expect him to be interested in them, he had propped himself against a wall near the dance floor where conversation would be difficult and no one would suggest that he dance.

He'd been counting the minutes until he could politely leave, when an eager young blonde had latched on to him.

"Rhiannon Evans," she'd announced breathlessly. And she'd looked at him as if expecting him to know who she was.

She was young, definitely stunning and determinedly sparkling. "I'm an actress," she'd explained, forgiving him because he admitted he didn't know the first thing about movies. Wasn't really interested. Didn't watch them.

He should, she'd told him. He could start with hers.

She was getting billing now—"though still below the title," she admitted—and bigger and better parts. She told him she was serious about her craft and that she didn't want to be known simply for being beautiful—she said this last with no self-consciousness whatsoever—but for being good at her work.

There was an edge to her bright girlish chatter. Nick was

well-versed in female body language and he could see she had
An Agenda.

First there was the hand on his arm, then hers somehow
linked around his. She leaned into him. She patted his lapel,
then touched his cheek.

"I'm determined not to ride on my mother's coattails, either."
And that was when he'd learned she was Mona Tremayne's
daughter.

At least he knew who Mona was.

Nick doubted there was a male breathing who hadn't fanta-
sized about Mona Tremayne at some point in his life—her early
sex goddess movies had seen to that. Heaven knew as a young
man he had, even if she was nearly old enough to be his mother.

He'd met her a few days ago at a dinner Demetrios had hosted.
She'd been without her daughter then, thank God. Mona was
still strikingly beautiful, still worthy of fantasies if he'd been
so inclined. She was also warm and friendly, interested in what
he was doing at the palace.

When she learned he was here not for the wedding, but to
oversee the restoration of part of the palace, she'd said, "You
don't do ranches, do you?"

"Never have."

"You should consider it." She'd smiled encouragingly. "I've
got an old adobe on my property that needs to be restored before it crumbles back to primeval mud."

He'd laughed. But because old buildings of any sort interested him he'd asked her a few questions, then offered to send
her the names of some colleagues.

Rhiannon hadn't been nearly as interesting. But as she kept
on chattering. Nick contrived to look interested. At least she
didn't have marriage on her mind. He was sure of that.

There had been an edge of fragile desperation to her frenzied
chatter, and the way her gaze roamed the room, he thought she
was desperate for someone to see her with him.

He didn't mind who saw them together. Nothing was happening. Nothing was going to happen. And her presence kept the Savas matchmakers at bay.

Finally she paused and focused on him. "What do you do?" she asked.

And so he told her—at length—about architectural renovation and restoration. Served her right, he thought, for pawing him. It was clear that she didn't care a whit. She had other things on her mind.

So he droned on about beams and joists, about weight-bearing walls, about matching the plaster using original techniques. He talked about dry rot and rising damp and wormy floorboards—which in the interest of her further education, he offered to show her as he was currently engaged in pulling up some in the palace's east tower. He'd even gone so far as to say he'd taken a bedroom there so he could continue to work on the wormy floorboards at all hours.

He'd figured he might bore her enough that she'd go find someone more inclined to take her up on what she seemed to have in mind. Or maybe the suggestion would scare her off.

In fact, that was when she'd run her hand down his lapel, looked dreamily up into his eyes and told him how much she'd "simply adore" coming to his bedroom to see the renovations.

Nick began to think it might be a better idea to dance with her—and step on her toes.

But it hadn't come to that.

He'd been saved. By Edie Daley.

A less likely savior would have been hard to imagine. A less likely sister to the ethereally beautiful Rhiannon was hard to imagine, too.

They looked nothing alike. Though Nick supposed he could detect the Mona Tremayne cheekbones in both her daughters' faces. But the similarity ended there. Where Rhiannon determinedly emphasized those bones with makeup, Edie did nothing to highlight them at all.

The little makeup she wore seemed more designed to cover

up than accentuate. Though he suspected that what she was covering up were freckles.

He thought he would prefer the freckles.

He certainly preferred her flashing gray-green eyes and tart tongue to her sister's blue eyes and breathless babbling. Edie didn't charm, she didn't flatter. She didn't paw, either. She kept her distance.

And she got right to the business at hand, which was clearly making sure that her sister had nothing to do with him. Used to having women thrown at his head, Nick found Edie's portrayal of a determined mother hen, intent on extracting her chick from danger, oddly appealing. Her words to her sister, though, revealed that she understood that Nick was not the entire source of the danger. Clearly she realized that her sister was capable of disaster with very little help at all.

Nick didn't envy whoever Rhiannon's fiancé was. The poor guy would have his hands full with her—which made Edie's ability to direct her back onto the straight and narrow all the more impressive. Obviously she was a woman to be reckoned with.

She had presence. And character.

While she may not have had the perfect ageless features of her mother or the ethereal beauty of her younger sister, Edie had the kind of bone structure a camera would love, as well as the liveliest eyes he'd ever seen.

Nick liked lively eyes. He liked her take-charge, no-nonsense personality. He liked the fact that she was intent on backing away from him.

It made him want to get closer.

And once her sister had disappeared, Nick stopped trying to think of ways to escape the reception and instead tried to find ways to keep Edie Daley talking.

For the first time he began to enjoy himself as he drew her out, got her talking, even teased her a bit. She responded, then backed off. He didn't want her backing off.

So he asked her to dance.

The request probably shocked him more than it had her. Nick didn't dance. Hadn't for years.

The last woman he'd danced with had been Amy, three nights before their wedding, the night before she'd died. He'd danced with Amy and it had been the last time he'd held her in his arms.

It wasn't the same, he assured himself. Nothing like the same.

This was a one-off, a turn around the dance floor with a pretty, vivacious woman. He was at a wedding, for God's sake. Dancing was expected! Just because he hadn't done it in eight years… It meant nothing.

Dancing was only moving your feet to music. Hardly something to hold sacred. He should have done it years ago, would have if it had ever occurred to him.

So he was shocked again when Edie said no.

In all his thirty-three years Nikolas Savas had never been turned down for a dance—which was undoubtedly why he'd demanded, "Why not?"

Her unexpected, yet honest answer had made him laugh. Her feet hurt.

No woman he'd ever met—not even Amy—had actually admitted that those stupid pointy-toed shoes women wore hurt their feet.

When he'd knelt to ease hers off, they were so tight he couldn't believe she'd even got them on. He wasn't surprised when she'd said they belonged to her sister. No wonder she didn't want to dance. It was astonishing she could even walk.

But once he'd freed her feet and tossed the offending footwear under the table—so she wouldn't dare crawl under and rescue them—she let him take her into his arms and swirl her onto the dance floor.

It was like riding a bike. Once you learned how to dance, you never forgot.

But it wasn't like dancing with Amy.

Amy had been tiny, the top of her head barely reaching his

shoulder. Edie's nose would have bumped his chin if she'd come that close. She didn't. She kept her distance and periodically glanced down at her stocking-clad toes.

So did he. They charmed him. She seemed shocked by them. Shocked to be dancing with him.

But she moved well, except for the fact that every once in a while she would stiffen and start to pull away.

When she did, he drew her closer, enjoying the feel of her soft breasts against his chest, of the silky dark hair that brushed his jaw when she turned her head. He brushed his lips against her hair.

She stiffened again. "Are you staring?"

No, that wasn't what he was doing. He grinned. "No."

"You are, too. You're ogling my feet."

He laughed and pulled her even closer. "There. Now I can't see them. Better?"

"Er, um," she muttered into the wool of his lapel. He felt her body stiffen again, but she didn't pull away. And seconds later, the tension seemed to ease, her body settled against his as they moved together.

Much better, he decided. Except that his body was becoming increasingly aware of how very appealing she was. Nick might have sworn off the idea of marrying after Amy's death, but he hadn't sworn off sex.

And thoughts of taking Edie Daley to bed were very appealing.

She seemed to fit in his arms, and as they moved together, he rested his cheek on her hair. She had amazing hair, not at all like the straight platinum curtain Rhiannon wore. Edie's was thick and dark and wavy. He suspected it had started out the evening tamed by a pair of gold hair clips just above her ears. But it was a long while since those clips had done their job. Even as she danced, her hair was escaping, curling wildly with a life of its own.

He wanted to thread his fingers through it, bury his face in it. He imagined what it would look like spread out against the sheets. He began to consider again how to get her there when the last strains of the waltz died away and the orchestra segued into something louder, faster and with a pounding of drums, which matched the thrum of his blood coursing through his veins.

"Well," Edie said, abruptly drawing back and pulling her hand out of his. "That was nice."

Nice? Nick stared at her, jolted.

She nodded, dimpling as she smiled. "Very nice. Thank you for the dance." There was something almost impishly polite in her tone, as if she knew the effect she was having on him—and wasn't going to even give him a chance to try his moves.

But Nick wasn't going to give up without an effort.

"I can do better than nice," he promised, holding out his hand, silently urging her to take it, to come with him.

Resolutely Edie shook her head. "Thank you, but no. And it isn't impolite to refuse a second dance," she informed him before he could claim otherwise.

"How about a glass of wine? We can sit this one out."

But again she shook her head. "It's been a pleasure, Mr. Savas. Thank you for being kind to my sister. And thank you for the dance. I...enjoyed it."

Had he heard an infinitesimal hesitation in her words? Before Nick could decide, Edie held out her hand and shook his politely. "Good night."

No!

He didn't say it. Blessedly his mouth stayed firmly shut. But a thousand things ran through his mind that he might say to stop her, to prolong the moment, to keep her there.

That he wanted to so badly surprised him. He wasn't used to feeling any such compulsion. Didn't *want* to feel it.

Bedding her, yes, he'd like to do that. But just keep her there to talk to him? There was no point.

So he tucked his hands into his trouser pockets and nodded.

"Good night, Ms. Daley," he said equally politely. "Thank you for the dance."

She turned away. But as she did so, he couldn't resist. "If you ever do want to see the architectural renovations in my bedroom, Ms. Daley…"

She spun back, her eyes flashing green fire.

Nick's heart kicked over. He turned on his best million-megawatt come-hither grin. Edie turned and, with a toss of her head, disappeared into the milling dancing crowd.

Only when the crowd had swallowed her up did he turn away. He felt oddly flat.

He should have gone back to his room then. It was nearly midnight. He'd done his duty. Showed up. Even danced. No one would remark on his vanishing now.

But he didn't go. He prowled the edges of the dance floor, restless and out of sorts. Edgy. Hungry. And not for food. His body was still aware of how neatly Edie Daley had fit into his arms.

"Damn it." Abruptly he turned and asked the nearest unattached female for a dance.

Why not? He'd danced once tonight already. It was just more of the same.

But it wasn't the same. This woman was nothing like Edie Daley.

She didn't settle into his arms with a reluctance that gave way to rightness. She plastered herself against him, locked her fingers together behind his neck and nibbled on his jaw. She didn't so much dance as slither and move against him until at last the music ended and Nick was finally able to peel her off again.

"Another?" she murmured.

"No." He'd had enough. More than. "I'm done dancing," he said firmly, though years of having good manners drilled into him made him try to look regretful as he stepped away. "I'm calling it a night."

Even as he did so, someone's hand touched his arm from behind. "I'm glad to hear it," an unexpected female voice said.

Nick spun around—and stared with shock into Edie Daley's gray-green eyes. She linked her arm firmly through his and gave him a blinding smile. "Because I've just decided that I'd love to see those architectural renovations."

CHAPTER TWO

NICK'S brows shot up. So did his heartbeat. And the spark of interest that had vanished when she had was back in spades.

But even as his libido was in favor of her suggestion, his brain was saying, *Hang on a minute.*

"Change your mind?" he asked her, careful not to sound too eager even though he damned well was.

Edie's smile, if possible, grew brighter. "Yes." Her voice was firm and clear. No hesitation at all. But he spotted a glitter in her eyes that he hadn't seen before. And was that a bit of her sister's desperation in her tone? He narrowed his gaze on her.

Her lashes flickered rapidly. Her smile amped up a bit more. Yes, this was desperation. And defiance, too. He could see that now. But exactly who or what had inspired it, he had no idea.

Carefully he let out a breath, drew another as he studied her from her flyaway hair to the tips of her stocking-clad toes. He wanted to take the stockings off those toes.

Would she let him?

Whatever was going on, taking her to his bedroom couldn't be a bad thing. Could it?

Nick guessed he'd find out.

Putting his hand over hers, he smiled down at her. "By all means." Then he turned to the blonde he'd danced with, the one who was still standing there and whom he'd completely forgotten about. "Thank you for the dance," he said to her politely. "Good night."

Then he laced Edie's fingers through his and started to lead her back to where they'd first met.

"The door is that way." Edie was practically dragging her feet.

"Shoes," he said and dived beneath the table. The miserable things were still there. He grabbed them and rose again, then slanted Edie a glance.

"You don't want to wear them, do you?"

She laughed, but it was a more brittle laugh than she'd shared with him before. Something had indeed happened. "I certainly don't," she said.

Nick tucked the shoes in his coat pockets so only the spiky mauve heels protruded. Then he offered her his arm. With no hesitation at all, Edie linked her arm through his and walked, head held high, along beside him, her bearing more regal than the queen of Mont Chamion.

Her posture was stiff and far more tense than when they'd danced, and she didn't speak again. But Nick knew better than to ask about it now. Edie kept her gaze straight ahead until they had nearly reached the door.

Then, near the door they came upon Mona and the small but inevitable knot of men clustered around her. Edie barely glanced their way, but she turned her gaze on him, focused a melting smile right at him and fluttered her lashes.

Nick almost laughed. He did smile at raised brows on Mona's face. There was a look of surprise and something else—consternation?—on Edie's mother's face. Whatever had sparked Edie's return, it had something to do with her mother.

Or, Nick realized as Mona said something to the man standing next to her who was staring at Edie and frowning, did it have something to do with him?

He was about Nick's age, fair-haired and handsome in a young Robert Redford sort of way. Familiar looking, but Nick couldn't put a name on him.

An actor, no doubt. Actor friends of Demetrios's were thick on the ground tonight.

This one transformed his frown into an engaging grin and stepped forward to intercept them as they approached. "Edie! Long time no see. I was so glad when Mona said you were here."

Edie's fingers tensed against his arm, but she smiled, too. "Not here for long," she said, still moving. "We're just leaving."

"But we haven't danced."

She kept smiling, but Nick could see it was tight. "Nice to see you again, Kyle. Good night."

"I'll see you in the morning, then," the man called Kyle said.

But they were already past him and headed toward the door when Edie said brightly to Nick in tones that were certainly loud enough to be overheard, "Which wing is your room in?"

Nick didn't think he imagined the sound of several people sucking air behind them. His own brows arched, but he said cheerfully, "I'll show you," gave her a melting smile for good measure and held the door so she could sail through it ahead of him.

Only when the door closed behind them did Edie seem to sag. But almost at once she pulled herself up straight and tall again, and kept right on walking until they'd left the reception area totally and were in one of the long walnut-paneled corridors. There at last she stopped and took a deep breath, then looked up at him.

"Thank you," she said, all her previous brightness gone. But the brittle tone had vanished, too.

Nick liked that. "My pleasure." She looked pale suddenly and he said, "Do you need to sit down?"

She gave him a wan smile, but shook her head. "I'm all right."

Still she looked rattled. Not at all like the Edie Daley who had come running to defend her baby sister. "What am I missing?" he asked her.

She looked down at her feet, then rubbed the bottom of one stocking-clad foot against the top of the other. They looked as vulnerable as she did. He wondered if she was going to deny that he was missing anything.

But at last she looked up at him and made a wry face. "My mother's heavy-handed attempt at matchmaking, I fear."

"The blond guy with the hundred-dollar haircut?"

Edie looked startled, then sighed and nodded. "Yes."

"You're not interested in him?" Nick was surprised how glad he was to hear it.

"No!" she said with a force that indicated more than indifference. She seemed to realize it because she muttered, "I'm not. I was just—I was afraid she'd try something like this."

"She being your mother?"

Edie nodded.

"She often sets you up?"

"She hints."

"And you don't like that?" He supposed she had a right to dislike matchmaking relatives as much as he did. But most women he knew welcomed the meddling. "Matchmaking is a bad thing?"

"Yes, it is," Edie said flatly. She didn't elaborate at first, and he thought she was going to change the subject. But then she sighed, "She thinks I need to start dating again."

"Again?" Nick prompted when she didn't explain.

There was another pause, as if she were deciding how much to say. Finally she looked around, then back at him and said impatiently, "Where are these architectural renovations?"

His brows lifted. "You really want to see them?"

"Do they really exist? Or were you flirting with my sister?"

"They really exist. And I wasn't flirting with your sister. Coming to see them was her idea."

"But you invited me—"

"I was flirting with *you*." And not giving her a chance to respond, not waiting to see what her reaction to that actually was, Nick grasped her hand in his and led her toward the tower.

She didn't speak as they walked, and Nick didn't say anything, either. He was too busy trying to assess the situation, trying to decide if she had been merely using him to avoid an unpleasant confrontation, no more no less? Or had she been angling for something else considerably more intimate.

He knew which he would prefer.

What she wanted he guessed he'd find out, he thought as he stopped and unlocked the east tower wing door. There was no one else staying in it but him so he'd only left a few lights burning, and the hall was cast in gloom when he pushed open the heavy door.

Edie paused at the entrance to peer into the shadows.

"Having second thoughts?" Nick asked. He wouldn't have blamed her.

But she took a quick breath. "No." There was a moment's pause and then she turned her head and met his gaze. "Are you?"

The question caught Nick off guard.

He'd slept with other women since Amy's death. It had been eight years, after all, and he had never claimed he would be a monk.

But it hadn't meant anything. Not the way it had with Amy. It was an itch he scratched. But only with women who considered it the same way he did.

He looked intently at the woman beside him now and wondered how Edie Daley considered it—she who wasn't even dating. That was when he realized that she was still looking at him, waiting for an answer.

Quickly Nick cleared his throat. "No," he said just as firmly as she had.

Edie smiled. It wasn't the smile she'd given her mother or the man named Kyle. It wasn't the brittle smile she'd given him when she'd reappeared and taken his arm. It was the smile he'd coaxed out of her before they'd danced—a genuine smile, he thought, and one that wasn't reluctant. It sent a shaft of desire right through him.

He wanted more of those smiles. More of her.

"Let me show you my renovations," he said, and he began to talk about the structure of the building. Several sentences later he realized that she was staring at him, wide-eyed, and he stopped. "What?"

"You really know all this stuff?" She sounded amazed.

Nick laughed. "It's what I do. My job. Why I'm here."

"I thought...the wedding..."

"I didn't come for the wedding. I came to restore the east tower."

And suddenly the smile he'd been hoping for lit her face. "How wonderful," she exclaimed. "Show me. Tell me everything."

He thought she might just be being polite, but as he turned on more lights and walked her through the main rooms, which were already finished, all the time telling her about the history of the place, explaining when it had originally been built and which parts were added on later, she asked eager, interested questions.

She didn't endure his lecture as her sister had done, but demanded to know more. Of course, to be fair, he'd deliberately droned on when he'd described his work to Rhiannon. He took pains to interest her sister.

But it wasn't long before he realized he needn't have bothered. Edie was clearly interested in the castle and in the work he'd done on it. She had studied history in college, she told him. She'd thought she might be a teacher.

"A teacher? Far cry from being your mother's business manager, isn't it?"

Her lips twisted. "One of those times when life happened while I was making other plans."

What plans? Nick wondered, but he didn't ask as there was something in the expression on her face that told him to leave it alone. So instead he asked, "Did you ever want to go into acting?"

She shook her head. "Never. That's not my world."

"But you work in it every day."

"In the business part of things. Not the glitz and glamour part. Not the movie star bit," she said adamantly.

"You don't like the 'movie star bit'?"

"It's not for me," she said simply, then added, "it's too difficult."

"Acting?"

"I suppose that's part of it. But I think really that it's harder being real. Being honest. If you act all the time, who are you? Really? Do you even know?"

Her voice rose when she asked the questions and they didn't sound rhetorical. Nick supposed, having a mother who was an icon of American film and screen, she'd probably given it considerable thought. Then, as if she decided she'd betrayed a bit too much emotion, Edie shrugged and said lightly, "I'm a behind the scenes person, that's all."

"Yeah. Me, too." When she blinked, clearly surprised, Nick explained. "When I'm working on a building, the building is what matters." He waved a hand to encompass the whole of the one he'd been working on. "Not who does the work."

Edie looked thoughtful, then she nodded. "Yes. I see what you mean." Then she ran an appreciative hand down one of the window casings. "You've done an amazing job. At least I guess you have. Honestly, it's hard to tell where the old stuff ends and the new begins."

"Exactly the way it's supposed to be."

"How do you start?"

"I case the joint," he told her with a grin. "I go over it all with a fine-tooth comb, so to speak. I learn who built it and when and why. Then I live in it."

"Hence the architectural renovations in your bedroom," she said with a grin. "Seriously?"

"Seriously." He pointed toward a door at the far end of the hall. "My digs."

Her gaze followed his gesture. Rhiannon would doubtless have rubbed up against him and suggested, "Show me."

Edie looked at the door, then turned back to him and asked, "When was the tower built?"

So Nick told her.

"It was a thirteenth century addition to the castle. It was designed to be a lookout and barracks for the soldiers who defended against the onrushing hordes."

"Hordes?" Her eyes got wide. "There were hordes? It's so small! Why would they bother?"

"The whole country was bigger back then. The royal family had more wealth and they had some good mountain valleys for cultivation. There are several natural springs as well as rivers. It would have made a nice prize for whoever could take it." He grinned and shrugged. "But no one could."

"I had no idea."

"The Chamion family are survivors. They knew how to pit one enemy against another. They also knew how to make alliances and how to make friends. There's lots of history here," he went on as he led her through the finished rooms to a heavy oak door at the far end. He pushed it open to reveal a hall where there was substantial scaffolding. "We're still working in here."

There were tarps and sawhorses—his concession to modern working conditions—all over, along with piles of lumber. But the tools were all primitive, ones that thirteenth century carpenters, joiners and masons would have used. Edie headed straight for them. She asked about every one, made him explain how he used them, where he'd found them. She looked at him with admiration when he said he often made his own.

"A matter of necessity," he said. "No old ones left."

"And you do it all yourself?"

Nick laid a proprietary hand on one of the scaffolds. "I started it. I did the first rooms on my own so I had a good feel for things. Recently I've been working up in the tower and there are a couple of local craftsmen doing this."

She walked around the room, noting where he'd replaced a joist. The new wood was evident. But she ran her finger over the chisel marks and shook her head. "It must take forever."

"Which is why it took generations to build places like this."

She smiled, then lifted her gaze from the wood to look at him again. He felt her gaze assessing him. "You look like such a 'modern' man," she said. "It's hard to imagine you spending your days doing this."

His mouth quirked. "Well, I don't usually wear a suit to work."

"How did you get into it? Kids usually say they want to be a fireman or a cowboy."

"I wanted to be an architect."

"Of old buildings?"

He shrugged. "I like them."

"Have you ever designed a new building?"

"Once," he said curtly, turning away.

There was a moment's silence. Then, "I'm sorry," Edie said.

Nick shot her a quick glance from beneath drawn down brows. She was leaning against one of the worktables, her gentle eyes on him, looking incongruous and desirable, both at the same time. "Sorry about what?" he said gruffly.

"Getting too close."

His frown deepened. "Close to what?"

"You." She smiled faintly. "Asking about how you came to do this. What you had designed," she added.

He felt an edginess between his shoulder blades. "It's not important." He picked up a chisel and balanced it on his palm, stared at it, then abruptly set it down again to look at her.

She looked back, her brows lifted a little. "I would have said it was very important," she countered quietly.

She would have been right.

Now Nick rubbed the back of his neck, kneaded the muscles, but they remained tense. "It was," he said tonelessly. It had changed his life.

This time she didn't ask. She didn't pry. She simply waited.

Nick shoved his hands into his trouser pockets, rocked back on his heels, stared into the middle distance, not at Edie.

"I designed a house," he said at last, unsure why the words were coming out of his mouth. He didn't talk about the house. Had never talked about it with anyone. But now he found himself saying, "I was getting married. I built it for my fiancée." He said the words almost defiantly.

Edie made a small sound. Otherwise she didn't move, didn't speak.

"It was supposed to be the perfect house," he went on, his tone as harsh as his feelings. He'd intended it to be his gift to her. He'd wanted it to be perfect. As perfect as she was.

Amy had laughed at that. "Don't be silly," she'd said. "I'm far from perfect."

But he'd thought she was. Absolutely perfect in every way. She was certainly perfect for him.

So he'd made her tell him everything she'd ever dreamed of having in a house—the expansive picture windows looking out across Long Island Sound, the winding staircase, the second-story balcony overlooking the naturally landscaped pool. The massive stone fireplace, the island-centered kitchen, the three upstairs bedrooms—a suite for them and one each for the children they would have—he was determined they would all be exactly as she wanted them.

"Her heart's desire," he said bitterly now.

"But it wasn't?" Edie ventured softly.

He shrugged. "She didn't care. Oh, she was delighted about the house, thought it was a great idea. But mostly she just wanted to get married. And I kept putting it off. I wanted the house finished. I wanted it all just right."

Not because he didn't want to marry her. He had. But he'd wanted to give her the very best he had to offer. He'd thought it was worth waiting for.

He'd been wrong.

The inadequacy of that house compared to the time he could

have had with her still gutted him. He ground his teeth, cracked his knuckles. Swallowed hard.

"What happened?" Edie asked quietly.

"She died."

He said the words baldly. Forced himself to confront the mistake he'd made. He didn't look at Edie. This wasn't about her. It was about him. And Amy.

For a long moment Edie didn't say anything, either. Nick wasn't surprised. What, after all, was there to say?

He should have kept his own mouth shut. He couldn't imagine what he'd been thinking, dragging out his private pain for a woman he'd known less than a couple of hours.

"Forget it," he muttered. "I shouldn't have said anything."

"I asked." She reached out, touched his arm. "I am so very sorry," she told him.

A lot of people had said they were sorry. But Edie's words didn't sound like a platitude. He could hear the earnestness in her voice, and there was something so close to pain in her tone that it surprised him. He turned to look at her.

"You lost her," Edie said, "and you lost your own future as well."

"Yes." It was something that no one else seemed to get. He wasn't the one who had died, after all. He should just get on with his life. If they didn't say it—and some did before many months had passed—he could see it in the way they looked at him, in the suggestions for dates, in the offers to set him up with eligible women.

"I understand," she said.

He doubted it. "Thank you," he said politely and looked away out the window.

"My husband died two years ago."

Nick's gaze snapped back, shocked, to meet hers. His "I'm sorry" felt as feeble and inadequate as a platitude now. "I didn't know."

"I don't generally announce it," Edie said lightly. Then she gave him a faint smile. "I don't suppose you do, either."

"No." It had been, literally, years since he'd talked about Amy to anyone. Now he paused, considering. "That was why you were upset about Mona's matchmaking?"

She thinks I need to start dating again. Nick remembered Edie's earlier words. Remembered wondering about the *again.* Now he knew.

She hesitated, then nodded. "Yes."

He understood. It made perfect sense. He didn't look at her. He didn't think she was looking at him. She was probably thinking about the husband she'd lost much more recently than he'd lost Amy.

And he was thinking about—her. About Edie.

He tried to think about her as someone's wife. He wondered what had happened, didn't feel as if he could ask.

She wasn't that close to him. Three feet, maybe even four. But even without looking he could feel her presence. There seemed to be a hum of awareness between them. Or maybe it only went one way. However it went, Nick felt a connection. He wanted to soothe away her pain, make her forget.

But he knew better than anyone that you didn't forget.

Now he heard her move, step away from the side of the table and he turned to face her again. She was smiling, but it was a faint smile. Sad, he thought. And why not? She had reason to be sad.

"I should go," she said now. "I've intruded on you enough."

But as she moved past him toward the door, he caught her arm. "Don't," he said. And when she looked up into his eyes, he said, "Stay."

Just one word. Low, rough, but laced with an urgency that surprised him. The very word surprised him. The request. The command.

He didn't know what to call it. Only knew he didn't want her to leave.

Edie looked surprised, too. Her lips parted, but for a moment no words passed through them. She seemed to be weighing her answer, deciding how to respond. Finally she said lightly, "You're not done with the tour yet?"

The question allowed them both to back off. Nick nodded. "You haven't seen the tower."

"The tower?" she echoed.

"I've been redoing the stairway up to the parapet, rebuilding the tower and the battlements. There's a fantastic view. You should see it." But he said wryly, "You're not exactly dressed for it." She was, of course, still in her stocking feet.

"I'll risk it," she said promptly.

"I'd carry you, but the passage is too narrow."

"It's all right. I can climb."

"The stones are too rough. Hang on. I'll get you something to wear on your feet."

He strode down to his own room and came back moments later with a pair of his flip-flops. He grimaced. "They're too big. But if you really want to do it, they're better than nothing."

"I really want to do it."

So did he. He crouched down to put the flip-flops on her, then realized at the same time she did that she would have to shed her stockings first.

There was a moment's pause. Edie's toes curled, then a second or two later slowly straightened again. Nick's mouth felt suddenly dry.

"Let me help you," he offered, lifting his gaze to her face.

It was shadowed. Her expression was hard to read, but he saw her touch her tongue to her lips. Then she bit down on the lower one and, looking down at him, held perfectly still.

He took that for agreement. "Hang on," he instructed her, and hoped to God he could do the same.

It was hardly the height of intimacy, sliding his fingers up beneath her dress to find the tops of her stockings or panty hose or whatever she was wearing.

On the other hand, it was pretty damned erotic. The stockings felt like real silk, smooth and warm against her legs, so fine that he was afraid his callused fingers would snag them.

So he proceeded slowly, trying to be careful, to move lightly. But the hint of firm flesh beneath that silken barrier was enticing. He loved to touch. He wanted to stroke as his hands snaked over her calves, past her knees, up her thighs. He could feel her legs tremble.

Fingers suddenly clutched his head, gripping his hair. He sucked in a breath. "S-sorry," she muttered. Her fingers loosened their grip, then as his continued their journey, hers tightened again. They sent a shiver down his spine.

But that sensation was nothing compared to the shaft of desire that shot straight to his groin as the silk beneath his fingers turned to lace and then, an inch later, to warm bare skin.

Nick sucked air, then tried to steady his breathing, to be matter-of-fact. This wasn't a seduction—unless he was the one being seduced.

Now he hooked his fingers inside the top of one stocking and drew it down, then slipped it off her foot. Then he skimmed his fingers back up the other leg. But knowing what he would encounter didn't make it any easier to feign indifference.

He *wasn't* indifferent. And when he stood up—provided he could manage to stand up—she would know it.

So he took his time, sliding her feet into the flip-flops, then picking up the stockings and folding them.

"I'll do that." Edie nearly snatched them out of his fumbling hands. Hers seemed to be full of thumbs as well. But at least her focus on them allowed Nick to wince his way to his feet and adjust his trousers so that his reaction was not immediately obvious.

He cleared his throat. "Right. We can go up this way." He picked up the flashlight on the worktable and headed toward a door at the far end of the room. "Be careful."

* * *

If she were being careful, Edie thought, she wouldn't be here now. She'd be back in her room listening to the faint sounds of the orchestra through the open window while she read a book.

But she wasn't. She was climbing a steep, winding, extremely narrow stone staircase behind a man who had just slid his hands up her legs. Her body was still tingling from the touch of his fingers. Her brain was still jangled from a hormone overload after over two years of complete disinterest. And her emotions were as unreliable as a teenager's. She *should* be in bed with a book—preferably one that would bore her to sleep!

Instead here she was trying to keep her eye on the beam of the flashlight that Nick was aiming at the steps as he climbed. He had angled it so that she could see it playing against the stairs and the wall without having to watch it through his legs.

But she preferred to study his legs.

She tried not to—and that was when she stumbled.

"Oh!" She gasped as her foot slipped. She reached out to grab at the side of the wall as she felt her footing fail. But before she could grab anything, Nick had spun around and grabbed her.

He hauled her up against him so that she was sure he could hear the pounding of her heart. She could certainly hear it. Or maybe that was his.

"Are you all right?" he demanded. Then, without waiting for an answer, because surely he could feel that she was fine—after all that was her body pressed against his—he said, "This is insane. I never should have brought you up here."

It might be insane, but climbing the stairs wasn't what made it so.

"I'm all right," Edie said. "Truly."

He made a sound that implied he wasn't convinced. If she lifted her face just a little, Edie thought her lips could probably brush his jawline. She couldn't see, of course. Other than the flashlight, which was now behind her in the arm he had wrapped around her, there was no light at all. And yes, his heart was hammering, too.

"You're sure?" He asked after a moment.

Edie nodded. She was right. The top of her head collided with his chin. "Sorry. Yes, I'm okay. I just slipped. Please, let's go on."

He didn't immediately agree, but finally he said, "Okay. But you're going ahead of me." And he eased her up the narrow stairway so that she was in front of him. Then, keeping one arm around her, playing the flashlight on the steps just ahead of her, he climbed the steps directly behind her.

He was so close his knees brushed her calves, so close she could feel the warmth of his breath against her back. And his other hand, big and warm and callus-roughened, wrapped her fingers. She'd wondered about the calluses when they were dancing. She understood how he got them now.

She remembered the feel of them sliding up her legs and touching the bare skin of her thighs. She wondered how those hands would feel against more sensitive skin on her body.

Once more she stumbled. Nick tightened his grip. "Careful."

"Yes," Edie said, breathless and mortified, taking another step and then another. "I'm trying to be."

Was she? Or was she actually being more reckless than she'd ever been in her life? She didn't know the answer to that yet.

"One step at a time," her grandma Tremayne always used to say. "You'll get there that way."

Edie supposed it was true. But it would have helped if she'd known where she was going.

"Here we are." They had reached a heavy wooden door. Nick reached around her and pushed open, then drew her up and out onto the narrow walkway.

"Oh!" Edie stopped stock-still and simply stared at the sparkling kingdom spread at her feet.

If the evening had felt like something out of a Cinderella fairy tale before, now, with the tiny lights of Mont Chamion's formal gardens spread out below her, Edie felt herself swept ever more fully into a sense of enchantment.

"Not exactly what it would have looked like in the thirteenth century," Nick said wryly.

"But beautiful," Edie murmured, putting her hands on the rough stone wall and leaning out to look down. "It's amazing. We have gardens back at home in Santa Barbara. But nothing like these."

"There aren't any like these. They're one of a kind." Nick's voice was quiet, almost reverent, as he came to stand beside her and together they stared out at the wonderland below. Neither of them spoke.

There were a few wedding guests outside in the gardens, and Edie could hear an occasional murmur of a voice or crack of laughter. From an open window came the lilting sounds of the orchestra playing a waltz. But as magical as it was, it was less enthralling than the man next to her.

He stood very close, but not touching her as he leaned forward, his elbows on the wall, the pristine white of his shirt cuffs peeking out from beneath his dark suit coat. His fingers were loosely knotted together. In the light of a three-quarter moon, she could, glancing sideways, see the light and shadow on the hard angles and planes of his face.

Her sister Rhiannon had casually and flirtatiously stroked his cheek. Edie's fingers curled into a fist so she wasn't tempted to do likewise. She turned her gaze away, too, tried to focus on the tableau below.

What Nick was actually thinking she didn't know. While moments ago in the stairwell she would have said he was as aware of her as she was of him, now he seemed so remote she doubted he was thinking about her at all. So she turned her head to risk another look.

He turned at the same time. Their gazes locked. The heat flared. And Edie's breath caught in her throat.

Nick cleared his. Then, deliberately he straightened. "It's getting cool up here. Shall we go down?" His voice was perfectly polite, but Edie thought she detected a hint of raggedness in his tone. The raggedness of desire?

Did she even know what that sounded like anymore?

"I'll go first on the way down," Nick decreed.

"So I can crash into you and knock us both all the way to the bottom?" Edie joked.

"Hang on to my shoulder if you want. I'll go slow."

He did go slow, but she didn't reach for him. She might have liked a hand, but clutching at him unnecessarily was something Rhiannon would have done, so Edie deliberately didn't do it. She just kept one hand on the wall as she made her way carefully down the steps behind him and tried not to stumble and crash into him. It was a relief to reach the hallway again and to have Nick turn and secure the door.

"That was lovely. Thank you," she said, slipping the flip-flops off and holding them out to him, smiling up at him at the same time.

Nick didn't smile back. His features were taut; there was almost a grim line to his mouth which, after a moment, he managed to curve into something resembling a smile. Then he stepped back and said briskly, "Well, there you have it. Nick Savas's two-bit architectural tour." He flashed her a quick glib sort of smile.

Edie's smile didn't flash. It remained firmly in place. But her heart was galloping and she had the sensation of walking on water. She dared not contemplate it too closely. She just needed to keep going. "It was wonderful."

Their gazes locked again. Nick's expression wasn't remote now. His eyes were intent. Focused on her. The silence went on. And on.

Until finally Nick said, "I want you."

His voice was rough. She heard an edge to it, a desperation almost. And something that sounded like annoyance. Edie wasn't annoyed. But she was shocked to hear him say the words so bluntly. At the same time, to her own astonishment, elated.

"Is that a problem?" she asked, keeping her tone light.

"Isn't it?" he challenged her, one brow lifting.

She blinked at the ferocity of his tone. "We're adults," she heard herself say mildly.

"There's more to it than that."

"Yes." She nodded, unsure where he was going with this.

"Usually," he amended.

Edie shook her head, not following. "I'm not sure what you mean."

"I mean," he said firmly, "that I don't want anything more than that."

"Than sex?" Edie said, wanting to be clear.

His jaw tightened and he looked faintly discomfitted by her plain-speaking, but nodded. "Exactly."

So much for fairy tales, Edie thought.

But really, she wasn't expecting a fairy tale, either. She knew better. So why not be frank? Why not set out parameters?

If Kyle Robbins had done so years ago, she wouldn't have been expecting a proposal of marriage when he'd simply wanted to go to bed with her. She wouldn't have had her hopes raised merely to see them dashed.

"I don't do relationships," Nick continued to spell it out. "One night. That's it."

"Those are the rules?" Edie said, smiling.

Nick nodded. "Those are the rules."

Their gazes met again, clear and unblinking. No starry-eyed foolishness here, Edie thought. No romance. No hearts and flowers. No expectations.

"Okay," she said at last, drawing the word out even as she came to terms with the implications.

Nick's brow rose a fraction higher. "You're all right with that?" He sounded as if he didn't believe her. "You're sure?"

"Well, I'm not expecting a proposal of marriage," Edie said sharply.

Nick raked a hand through his hair. "Good," he said with obvious relief. "Because I'm not making one." He shuddered and shook his head. "Never again."

"One day you might—" Edie began.

But he cut her off. "No," he said, absolutely adamant. "I won't."

Edie didn't think she ought to say she felt sorry for him, but the truth was, she did. She had loved Ben with all her heart and soul. But she would never say she wouldn't fall in love again, wouldn't marry again. She'd told Mona she wasn't interested because she hadn't been—then.

It didn't mean she wouldn't ever be.

Good grief, look how suddenly things could change. Two hours ago her hormones had been missing in action. She hadn't been remotely interested in a man. And now—now she was contemplating going to bed with a man she barely knew. Why? Because she was attracted to him, certainly. But mostly because she didn't trust herself not to do something even more foolish with a recently divorced, clearly interested Kyle Robbins. One night with Nick was far preferable.

"So if you're not interested, I'd completely understand," Nick was saying.

"I'm interested," Edie said. "One night. No relationship. Got it. That's what I want, too."

Nick stared at her long and hard.

Edie stared back, unblinking. *Don't look down. Don't look down.* The words echoed around her brain. Still he didn't move.

"I know what I'm doing," she assured him, with the slightest hint of irritation. "Do you?"

Apparently he did. Abruptly Nick closed the space between them and wrapped her in his arms.

Like when they'd danced, Edie thought for a split second.

But then as his hard, strong, warm body enveloped her in his embrace, she thought, *No, not like dancing at all.* A hundred, thousand, million times better.

Her whole body responded. Her knees wobbled. Her eyes

opened, then shut. Her lips parted and suddenly his mouth was on hers. Fierce, hungry, demanding.

I want you, Nick had said. His voice had been hungry, ragged.

But his subsequent words had seemed like some sort of impersonal negotiation of terms. There was nothing impersonal or negotiated about this. This was instinct, pure and simple. He was a man who wanted a woman—a man who wanted her.

And Edie wanted him, too. *Yes,* she thought, kissing him back. *Oh, yes!*

Yes, it was just one night. No, it wasn't going anywhere. She had no expectations. But where had expectations ever got her?

He wasn't Ben. But Ben was gone forever. He wasn't Kyle. And thank God for that.

He was Nick. And tonight—just tonight—he was hers. She was determined not to regret it.

CHAPTER THREE

SHE wasn't his usual sort of woman.

Nick didn't care.

He wanted her. And the desire that had been building all evening was the only thing that mattered to him now. She was tart and sweet, eager and tentative, cool and yet capable of burning him down to the ground.

She looked too closely, saw too much. And she wasn't afraid to talk about what she saw.

But they weren't talking now, were they?

No. They were kissing. God, yes, they were kissing! And her lips were as hungry as his. Her hands were as eager as his. They slid up his arms and around the back of his neck to hold his face to hers. He didn't complain. It was what he wanted, too.

Restless and eager, his hands roved over her back, tangled in her hair, loosening whatever pins she had anchored it with so that it fell in loose, heavy dark waves over her shoulders and down her back. He ran his fingers through it, buried his face in it, drew in the citrusy scent of shampoo and something exclusively Edie Daley.

It was heady, dizzying, and it didn't matter if she wasn't the sort of woman he ordinarily took to bed, a woman he could scratch a physical itch with and walk away from. He could do the same with her. He *would* do the same.

But first he would spend the night with her.

And yes, he knew exactly what he was doing.

"I missed a spot on the tour," he murmured against her lips.

Edie pulled back slightly, stared at him, disbelieving.

"My bedroom."

She smiled. Then she placed her hands on his arm and looked up into his eyes. "What a very good idea," she said. And there was a breathless quality in her voice that cranked his desire up another notch.

"Right this way." And he scooped her up into his arms and carried her down the hall to the room he'd been using as a bedroom, pausing only to kick the door open. Then he bumped it firmly shut again with one hip and then, in the darkness, lowered her onto his bed. He dropped down beside her, intending to pick up where they'd left off.

"Turn on the light," Edie said.

He pulled back and looked at her. "What?"

"If I'm getting a tour, I want to see everything."

Which wasn't a bad idea at all. He very much wanted to see her as he made love to her. He grinned.

"Or maybe there aren't lights," she reflected. "Do you use candles for an authentic ambiance?"

"It's possible to use candles," Nick said. But he reached over and flipped on a bedside lamp. "When they give tours at night, I imagine they do. But tonight I think a lamp will do."

It was a subdued light, but even so it threw the room with its utilitarian furnishings and spartan double bed into a pattern of light and shadow. Hardly the sight of a romantic seduction.

But Nick wasn't focusing on the room. He had eyes only for Edie Daley. He'd seduce her anywhere. She was half-reclining on his bed, the mauve dress dark against her creamy skin. The low light made Edie's peekaboo freckles entirely disappear and turned her skin to a soft gold while it made her dark hair look even thicker and more lustrous. Nick reached up a hand and ran his fingers through it again. It seemed to curl around his fingers with a life of its own. He rubbed a strand of it against his cheek, smoothed it over his lips, tasted it.

Then once more he buried his face into it, breathed deeply, knew the scent now—the hints of citrus and woods—and woman. This woman.

He wanted to give her a night to remember. He didn't want to erase her husband's memory. He knew she wouldn't forget just as he could never forget Amy. But equally, from here ever after, whenever Edie thought about making love, Nick wanted his face to come to mind.

He pulled back and undid his tie, then stripped off his coat and tossed it on the bureau. All the while he kept his gaze locked on hers. Smiling, Edie lay back against the pillow and watched him with a kind of hungry fascination that made his blood heat even more.

He reached for his shirt buttons, fingers trembling. As he did so, Edie raised a hand to touch his. "May I?"

Undress him? Nick wasn't used to giving up control. It seemed far too intimate. Risky. But Edie was smiling at him, looking hopeful, eager yet a little hesitant, too. And he knew he didn't want her hesitant. He wanted her to enjoy, to be involved, an active equal partner in their lovemaking.

So he gave a quick nod. "Be my guest."

Resolutely he dropped his hands to his sides and let her fingers do the work, certain his could have done in mere seconds. But the way they were trembling as she touched him, he wasn't sure that was true.

Edie sat up on the bed and leaned toward him, then began to studiously go to work on his shirt buttons. Her knuckles brushed lightly against the underside of his chin as she undid the top button. The soft brush of her skin against his made his chin tingle. As she moved lower, she caught her lower lip between her teeth as she concentrated on each one in turn.

His fingers clenched into fists to keep from pushing her hands away and doing it himself. It would be so much quicker and easier and he would get to feel her bare fingers on his skin that much sooner.

But having relinquished control he knew he couldn't wrest it from her now, knew she had to be the one to set the tempo.

So he let her—even as the tentative dance of her fingers damned near killed him.

Edie took her time.

She didn't know what was going to happen after tonight.

She didn't care. She didn't want to think about it. Since Ben had died, she'd spent too much of her life trying unsuccessfully to focus on the moment when she'd really never been able to do more than endure.

Not now.

Not tonight.

Not when this moment and those immediately following were going to be spent with Nick Savas—*making love* with Nick Savas.

She was going to savor it. Why not?

She'd missed the intimacy of the bedroom. Her first experience, with Kyle, had left her wondering what all the excitement was about. During the few weeks they'd been together, he had been fierce and hungry and demanding. He'd always directed things. Always taken charge. And with the eagerness of youth—he'd been twenty-three—Kyle had been more concerned with the end than the journey along the way. He'd never given her a chance to discover the subtleties of lovemaking.

With Ben it had been different. The two of them had learned together. They'd explored together. With Ben it had been about the journey, about pleasing, about loving, not simply about the orgasmic rush. It had been about knowing and being known.

She knew better than to expect that here. A single night meant nothing compared to the years she'd had with Ben. But until tonight she'd never even been tempted. She wasn't sure what that meant.

She wanted to find out.

Would she be in bed with him if Kyle hadn't turned up?

Probably not. Her well-developed common sense would likely have led her back to her room at a reasonable hour to her chaste single bed. And once there, then what? Would she have dreamed of Ben?

Lately she had not dreamed of him. For the past few months, she barely remembered dreaming at all. For all that she wanted to hang on to every memory, she knew he was slipping away from her. If she had gone to bed alone, would it have been memories of Ben that would have kept her awake? Or would she have tossed and turned all night thinking about this dark, handsome man who was holding so still now while she undid the buttons of his shirt.

The shirt was starched, the buttons stiff. It took a while. Edie enjoyed every moment.

It wasn't as if she was going to do it again, she told herself. Nick had been absolutely clear about that.

They were having a "one-night stand," she thought, and was appalled that those trite tawdry words could be used to describe what was happening at this very moment.

It didn't feel tawdry at all.

For all that it was unexpected, it felt—right.

So Edie shoved the words away, shoved all the rest of her life away, and focused on the man—and the moment.

She slid the last button loose, then eased the shirt off his shoulders and down his arms. Before she could decide where to go from there, Nick took it from her and tossed it aside. Then he yanked his undershirt out of his black trousers and started to pull it over his head.

Edie caught his hands. "Mine," she said, astonished at the word as it came out of her mouth.

Nick groaned, but he dropped his hands. "I get to undress you, then," he muttered, giving her a look that promised action.

"When it's your turn," she agreed, trying to sound as if it didn't make her shiver with anticipation. She was getting enough shivers just peeling his shirt over his head, then resting her hands for a moment on his shoulders before daring to rake her nails lightly down over his hair-roughened chest.

She could feel a tremor run through him as he remained still under her hands, his dark eyes hooded, watching her every move. She traced circles around his nipples, then arrowed her fingers down the center of his chest across his abdomen. They stilled when they came to rest at his belt.

"I suppose that's yours, too," Nick rasped, looking down.

Edie looked, too. "Sounds good to me," she said. "Do you want to stand up?"

He stood. She was just above eye level with the belt in question now. She brushed her fingers lightly over the front of his trousers as she began to undo the buckle. Nick drew a quick breath.

The buckle was easier than the buttons had been, and in bare seconds she had it undone. Without stopping to think about what she was doing, Edie skimmed down the zip of his trousers. Only when she did so, did she realize how close she was to the hot flesh that she wanted to touch, that she could tell, from its persistent press against the front of his shorts, wanted to touch her.

Belt undone, zip down, his trousers fell to the floor. Nick toed off his shoes and kicked them away, then stepped out of his pants and stood before her in only a pair of cotton boxers that did nothing to hide his arousal.

"Yours, too, obviously," he said gruffly, looking down. Then he lifted his gaze to meet hers. "Now it's my turn."

"I'm not done," Edie protested.

"Neither one of us is done," Nick said, grasping her hands in his, holding them loosely so she couldn't continue. "Let me catch up."

He bent his head and kissed his way down her bare shoulders, his hot mouth against her skin making her shiver as his fingers went to the back of her dress. Then he groaned and dropped his head against her shoulders.

"What?"

"There're five thousand buttons back here."

"Only forty, I think." But she remembered standing still for what seemed like forever as her mother had done up the dress. "Or maybe fifty."

"Fifty?" Another groan. But even as he did so, his nimble fingers set to work.

Nick Savas was a man of many talents, and he could multitask with the best of them, Edie thought, as his lips nibbled her jaw, her earlobes, her shoulders even as his fingers undid the buttons one at a time. Even his hair seemed to be actively seducing her as silky black strands brushed softly against her sensitized skin.

Then he sighed, pleased and lifted his head to smile at her. "Victory is mine," he murmured and hooked his fingers in the top of her dress and drew it slowly down.

The bra was part of the dress, and when he lowered the bodice, he bared her breasts. The cool air made her shiver. But so did the look on Nick Savas's face. Edie had never had the confidence in her bodily beauty that her mother and Rhiannon did. While she'd always known she had no major defects, she couldn't help feeling as if she suffered by comparison to her mother and sister.

But Nick seemed to be entranced by what he saw. His hands came up to cup her breasts, to weigh them gently in his hands. His thumbs rolled over her nipples heightening her awareness of her body's needs.

"Beautiful. You are so beautiful," he murmured and bent his head to lave first one breast and then the other. And Edie felt a shaft of desire clear to the center of her. She shivered.

"Are you cold?"

"N-no. I'm just—" But she couldn't seem to find words to express what she was feeling, so she just shook her head and savored the sensations.

Nick took his time as she had taken hers. He drew her off the bed, then as she stood before him, he pressed light kisses along her breastbone as he hooked his fingers inside the top of her dress, which was at her waist now. Kneeling, he continued to tug it down. The calluses on his fingers stroked her bare legs as he did so. She could still feel their imprint on her thighs from when he'd slid her stockings off. The dress pooled at her feet. He lifted first one and then the other, removing the dress completely. Then he skimmed the silk half-slip right down her legs, leaving her bare except for a pair of ecru lace bikini panties.

"Ah." He rested back on his heels and looked up at her. She could feel his gaze as it traveled slowly up her legs, past her belly, over her breasts to her face. He smiled at her.

He traced the lace at the top of her panties with a single tantalizing finger. Then he grasped them gently and pulled them slowly down.

Mindlessly Edie stepped out of them. Then, staring down at his head as he knelt before her, she felt his fingers begin at her ankles and stroke back up the length of her legs, teasing her smooth skin, making her tremble with need. Involuntarily she reached out and gripped his shoulders, hanging on for dear life.

His breath was warm on her belly. He kissed her there. Then his fingers slid slowly up the insides of her legs, reached the juncture of her thighs, brushed his fingers over the curls that covered her womanhood. Then he touched her there.

Edie swallowed a moan.

He didn't stop. On the contrary, he seemed to take it as invitation to go further, to part her legs and stroke between them. Her knees trembled. Her fingers tightened on his shoulders, dug into them.

"N-no f-fair."

He glanced up, smiling at her. "No?"

"You're not waiting for me."

He slanted her a glance. "Feel free to jump in anytime."

And so she did. Somehow he ended up on the bed beside her. Did she drag him there? Did he suddenly appear? She didn't know. She only knew that she couldn't get enough of him—even though, judging from the burgeoning of his shorts, there was a great deal of him. She hooked her fingers into the waistband of his boxers and dragged them down.

He shrugged them off, then settled beside her and began to explore her inch by inch. Edie was equally determined to take her time, to make this last, to wring every last moment of enjoyment out of the experience. But it wasn't easy because she was too eager, too hungry, too desperate.

Worse than Rhiannon, she thought.

But even thinking it didn't make her pull back. She wanted him. Her fingers dug into his hips as he settled between her knees. But still he took it slow, his fingers drawing light patterns of sensation as they moved up her thighs, brushed against her sex. His thumbs touched her, brushed her lightly, then slid back down her legs.

Edie swallowed a moan. She tried to lie still, not to squirm, not to lift her hips, not to seek his touch, not to betray how much she wanted him.

But he knew. He smiled, and his hands made the journey again. This time they traced small tantalizing circles on their way up, which he followed by pressing kisses first to the inside of one thigh and then the other. As he moved his head, his soft hair brushed against her sensitized skin. His lips were hot, but the moisture of his kiss was cool when he lifted his mouth and blew lightly where he'd just touched.

And every second he got closer. Closer.

Edie swallowed, tensed, waited, dug her heels into the mattress. Closer. Closer. Then his tongue touched her there—and she let out a little gasp.

"Nick!"

He lifted his head. "Yes?" Then he did it again. And again.

Edie's knees wobbled frantically, and her hands reached blindly to grab his hair. But she didn't pull away. She hung on. Desperate. Demented.

She twisted her head from side to side as he continued to stroke her, as his fingers followed his mouth, parting wet folds, sliding into her. His thumb found the most exquisitely sensitive spot and made slow firm circles as his fingers drove her mad with need. Her hips bucked.

"Oh!" She writhed on the bed. "Now! I—"

"Yes." The word hissed through his teeth. He kept one hand on her while he turned to the small cabinet by the bedside and took out a foil packet.

Protection. Edie understood. She was grateful he took the time and she helped him sheath himself, but she was almost equally grateful when, sheathed at last, he came to her, slid forward and slowly eased in, fitting exactly where he belonged, giving her exactly what she needed.

Instinctively Edie rocked up to meet him, dug her fingers fiercely into his buttocks and gave Nick what he needed, too.

She didn't know how she was so sure what he needed, but she was. Not just on a physical level—that wasn't hard to decipher at all. But on some other deeper instinctive level, she felt the connection between them.

She might have come to him for herself—to avoid the pull Kyle had always had on her emotions. But this had nothing to do with Kyle. This was only about the two of them—she and Nick as they moved together, slick and hard, eager and hungry, giving and taking in equal measure.

There was nothing tentative. No second thoughts. No thoughts at all. Just the sense of rightness—and completion.

They shattered together, breathless, weightless. Two made one.

And as he slid to the side and cradled her in his arms, Edie slept.

A few minutes. Half an hour, perhaps. But amazingly, she did sleep—deeply, dreamlessly—and when she awoke she felt remarkably refreshed as she snuggled in the smooth sheets and turned, coming up against a hard, warm body.

Nick Savas's body.

She felt a brief sense of shock. She waited for the feeling of impropriety. It wasn't there. Still she waited. It didn't come.

What came instead was a sense of satisfaction and an awareness of how good it felt to be with him. How right.

And how strange was that?

Edie didn't know. There seemed to be no limit to what she didn't know at the moment—like what she was supposed to do now.

Not get involved, she reminded herself.

Nick didn't want involvement. He didn't "do relationships." Well, yes. She'd gone into this with her eyes open. He hadn't led her on.

She wasn't changing the rules.

But somehow she wasn't prepared, either. The etiquette of the one-night stand was apparently beyond her. She'd never had one before.

She'd only slept with two men—Kyle and Ben. And with both she'd been in it for the long haul. Of course, Kyle hadn't been. But she hadn't known it at the time. And Ben had made her the happiest of women for their brief marriage. But he had wanted what she'd wanted: forever.

Whatever Nick Savas wanted, Edie was sure "forever" didn't come into it.

Probably he expected her to be sliding out of bed and out the door right now. But when she began to ease away, a strong arm curved around her and pulled her back into his arms.

"Where are you going?"

She turned her head to look at him. He was smiling at her, a lazy, satisfied smile. A smile she had put there, Edie reminded herself.

But even so, for the first time she felt a little awkward. "I should leave," she said tentatively.

"Why?"

"Because…" But the word trailed off and the reasons didn't

come. There were undoubtedly plenty of them, but none of them seemed as important as staying right here.

"Not good enough." Nick's smile became a grin. "Do you want to leave?" he asked.

She considered it again, thoroughly, and came to the same conclusion: she didn't want to leave at all. She liked being in Nick Savas's bed, liked letting her eyes drift over his handsome face, memorizing his features, the feelings, this moment. She wanted to bottle it and keep it even as she knew that was impossible.

But staying a little longer, that was possible. Slowly she shook her head.

"Good. We took the edge off," he said. Then he smiled. "Now we can take our time."

Which was exactly what he proceeded to do. He settled beside her and moved over her languidly this time, pausing to taste, to tease, to touch wherever it pleased him.

It pleased Edie, too. Kyle had never been the lingering sort. He'd never explored, never particularly been interested in what she wanted. Ben had been. But Ben was little more experienced than she had been. And while they'd learned together, they'd still had much more learning to do when Ben had died.

Since Ben she'd had nothing—felt nothing.

Until tonight.

Tonight she had Nick—and Nick had her. He was experienced. No doubt about that. But he wasn't self-centered. He wasn't going through the motions in order to get what he wanted. He was focused. He was involved, as intent on learning her secrets as he was on learning the details of these buildings he took apart and put back together again.

She felt as if he was doing the same to her.

The featherlight touch of his fingers as he explored her made Edie aware of nerve endings she hadn't even known existed. The graze of his tongue on the inside of her elbow made her shiver. The soft stroke of his thumb swirling around first one nipple and then the other made her breasts peak. The dance of fingers down the middle of her abdomen, then brushing lightly through the curls that hid the place that longed for his touch roused her senses, made her quiver.

She wanted him to hurry, to touch her, to find her and shatter her and make her whole again. At the same time she wanted it to last forever.

What Nick apparently wanted was to drive her insane.

His fingers moved back up her body again. She swallowed her desperation. Then he traced her ribs, swirled circles round her navel, then with his thumbs he caressed the juncture of her thighs. Edie bit her lip as his hands slid around beneath her to cup her buttocks. He lifted her, spread her, stroked her.

Edie nearly whimpered. "Now," she urged him, reaching out to grasp his hips and draw him to her.

He came to her then, thrust into her with a desperation belied by his earlier slow, leisurely caresses. There was nothing casual or leisurely now. His need, like hers, was naked and urgent. His teeth clenched. The skin drew taut across his cheekbones. His breathing grew quick and hard as did his movement. And Edie moved to meet him, to join him. She dug her nails into his back just as he gave a hoarse cry, and they shattered together again.

This time there was no edge taken off. There were no edges at all—just bone-deep contentment, relaxation, a sense of serenity and well-being as Nick's weight settled against her. He would have moved off. She held him where he was—wasn't ready to let go. Not now. Not yet.

Their hearts were still hammering in unison. His sweat-dampened cheek rested against hers. Midnight shadow whiskers abraded her sensitive skin. Instinctively Edie turned her head toward them, pressed her lips to his cheek, breathed in the scent of him.

Slowly he turned his head, too, so that they lay facing each other, sharing the pillow, their noses nearly touching, their eyes open, watching each other silently.

There were no words. At least Edie couldn't think of any. So she smiled. It said everything she couldn't find words for.

Nick didn't smile. He looked like a man who didn't know what had hit him. That made Edie's smile widen.

His eyelids flickered shut. He opened them again, seemed to focus on her once more. But within moments his eyes shut again, and this time they stayed shut. His breathing slowed and deepened.

He was asleep.

This time Edie didn't sleep at all. Her breathing, like Nick's, slowed and settled into a regular peaceful rhythm once more. But she felt no exhaustion now, no lassitude. She felt centered. Settled. Physically a little sore because she hadn't done this sort of thing in a while. But on the whole she felt astonishingly good.

Great sex will do that for you, she thought, remembering similar feelings after she'd made love with Ben. But with Ben it hadn't only been great sex. There had always been something more.

There had been a connection between them, the sense that together they made beautiful music, that together they created something greater than the two of them could on their own.

Could that happen with Nick, too?

The thought came from out of nowhere—or from some well-spring deep within. Edie didn't know where. She knew only that even thinking such a thing was a mistake.

Nick didn't want that. He'd made it absolutely, perfectly clear that he wasn't interested. And she had agreed to that. She'd assured him—and herself—that she wasn't interested in anything else, either.

She wasn't. She hoped.

And if she was?

Well, Edie acknowledged, that was her problem.

Now she lay quietly and allowed her gaze to trace Nick's sleeping features. He looked younger asleep, his hard features gentled. Was it the "great sex" that had softened them? Edie wondered. Or was it the great sex *with her?*

Had he felt the sense of connection, too?

Or—Edie forced herself to confront the possibility—was she just a lonely widow trying to rationalize a night of very uncharacteristic behavior?

She didn't have the answer to those questions. All she knew is that she wouldn't get those answers tonight. Maybe she never would.

But lying here was not helping. It was only making her want things she had no right to, with a man she didn't really know.

Except a part of her thought she knew Nick Savas very well indeed.

He had showed her tonight that it was possible to find life after Ben. And she certainly knew she would be thinking about him—and not about Kyle Robbins—for some time to come.

But now she needed to get up and get dressed and go back to her own room—to her own life.

There, over the next days or weeks or months, she might discover the answer to what she'd been doing tonight.

Carefully Edie eased herself from beneath his arm, then slipped out of the bed, wincing as she began to move about and gather up her clothing. Muscles she never knew she had were reminding her of their existence now.

In the bathroom—thank heavens for some modern conveniences!—she put on a small light and dressed as quickly as she could, which wasn't very as she had to slither into the dress since no one was available to button it up the back for her, and she could hardly saunter down the corridors of Mont Chamion castle with her dress hanging half open.

Fortunately it was still the middle of the night. Even the earliest risers would not be in the hallways just yet. But she had a plane to catch in a scant six hours.

So she slipped back out of the bathroom and started toward

the door, then stopped. She couldn't just leave—not without looking back. Not without one last memory.

So she crept back to the bed and stood over Nick's sleeping form, drinking in the sight of him. He'd rolled onto his back now. The sheet barely covered the essentials, but she had indelible muscle memory of them—and the soreness to remind her for a while at least.

Now she memorized the rest of him—the broad, hair-roughened chest, the strong shoulders, the blade-sharp nose, the sensuous lips, the hard planes of his cheeks, the delicate black half-moon lashes and the tousled dark hair. She wished she could see his eyes—sometimes laughing, sometimes haunted—again. The mirror of his soul.

Tonight he had touched her soul as well as her body. He had given her back a part of herself that had died with Ben. She hoped she had given him something, too. She took her time, imprinting him in her mind's eye now the way he had imprinted himself on her body during the night.

She looked. And looked. And then, because she couldn't help herself, she bent and brushed a kiss over his mouth. His lips moved, sought hers. But when she pulled away, when he didn't find her, his lips parted. He sighed.

Edie did, too. "Good night, Nick," she whispered. "Thank you." She allowed herself one last light touch on his bare shoulder. "I think."

And then she turned and slipped silently out into the night.

CHAPTER FOUR

THE unexpected sound of the front doorbell of her mother's Santa Barbara mansion startled her.

"Blast!" Edie shot a helpless glance in the direction of the living room, then turned a malevolent one on the computer screen she'd been staring at forever.

She was in the middle of making the latest of Rhiannon's many plane reservations. She was almost to the last screen. If she stopped now, it would "time-out" and she would have to start over.

God knew, she probably would anyway. Rhiannon had been changing things almost daily for the past two months. Ever since she and Andrew had had their meltdown in Mont Chamion, even though they'd made up, Rhiannon had been edgy and wired, worried about whether Andrew would dump her one minute, and whether her career was over the next. She was constantly changing her priorities and her mind, and today's rearranged schedule was just the latest indication of her turmoil.

It did not give Edie restful days, either. Fortunately Rhiannon was in the Bahamas shooting a music video today. If she hadn't been, chances were good she'd have been perching on the edge of Edie's desk talking a mile a minute, fretting about Andrew, and changing her mind even as Edie was rebooking her reservations. Now Edie glared at the hourglass, which still hung on the screen.

The doorbell rang again.

At its insistence, the dog, Roy, a gigantic Newfoundland—all black glossy fur and lolling red tongue—looked up with vague interest. As a pup he'd have been at the door already, barking like mad. Now at nine, he had a more casual approach to visitors. They had to be persistent or he wasn't interested. He lay his head between his paws and closed his eyes again.

The doorbell chimed again. Emphatically. Twice.

Well, whoever they were, Roy would give them points for persistence. Ah, at last. The new screen finally appeared asking her to confirm the ticket purchase. Edie clicked. The hourglass reappeared. She waited.

And the doorbell rang. Once, twice. Three times now.

Not many people got as far as Mona Tremayne's front door. Tucked away high in the mountains behind Santa Barbara, the acreage Mona had bought with Edie's father, Joe, was far off the beaten path.

Everyone else had urged Mona to move after Joe died. The acreage was too big, they said. It had been Joe's dream to have the cutting horse operation on rural Santa Barbara ranch land. But Mona had stayed true to that dream.

She and Joe had bought it not just for the horses, but because they'd wanted a place to get away to, a place where they could be themselves without coming face-to-face with the fanfare of Mona's growing celebrity on an hourly basis. Of course it hadn't had the present house on it then, only the now sadly decaying old adobe ranch house even farther from the road.

This house had come later, after Joe's death. In her grief Mona wouldn't leave the place they'd had together. But the crumbling old adobe was no place to be with two small children. Without Joe to keep things together, the roof would have fallen in on them at the very least. So Mona had had a new house built and a year later she and five-year-old Edie and nine-year-old Ronan had moved down the hill several hundred yards to what Ronan still called "Ma's movie star house."

It was big and lavishly decorated, parts of it definitely elegant

enough for spur-of-the-moment entertaining of Hollywood mo-
guls and the world's rich and famous. At the same time it had
eleven bedrooms, even more bathrooms, a butler's pantry big
enough for Edie's twelve-year-old twin half brothers Dirk and
Ruud to roller skate in, a swimming pool, tennis court and, oh
yes, a doorbell.

This time whoever it was didn't just ring it, they leaned on
it. Long and hard and far too shrilly.

Annoyed, Edie was tempted not to answer it at all. But Mona's
"open house" policy extended to whomever among her hundreds
of "close" friends turned up in the vicinity. Even when Mona
was on the other side of the world, she—or, basically, Edie—
welcomed all and sundry. The Tremayne hospitality was legendary, and Edie was quite happy to do it, though usually her
mother warned her before guests were expected.

Now the hourglass gave way to a "confirmed" screen.
Gratefully Edie punched a button to print Rhiannon's itiner-
ary, then, with Roy at her heels, she went to answer the bell—
which was still ringing

"All right! I hear you!" she shouted as she hurried down the
hallway from her office at the back of the house, across the living room and grabbed the handle of the oversize dark oak door.
"You can stop now!"

It stopped.

She jerked open the door. Her jaw dropped. Her fingers
clenched on the door handle. She stared in disbelief. *"Nick?"*

Because it was—Nick Savas in the flesh. As tall and gorgeous as she remembered. And as unexpected as—well, Edie
couldn't think of anything she had been anticipating less.

She clutched the door handle with one hand and Roy's collar with the other, as if they would anchor her in a storm. And
there was a storm—of emotions, of memories, of questions and
answers that she'd put behind her because she'd never managed
to sort them out.

Not that she hadn't tried. For weeks after she'd got back home after the wedding in Mont Chamion she'd thought about that night—about the man she'd spent it with. She thought about what she'd done and tried to understand why.

As near as she could come to an explanation was that somehow that night he had awakened her.

After two and a half years of going through the motions of getting on with her life—and yet never really finding the spark that would make her recognize that she was alive and fully functional again on all levels—that night she had.

Something—and she never did put her finger on what—about Nick Savas had touched something elemental in her. In her most fanciful moments she thought it was what the prince's kiss on Sleeping Beauty's lips had done—brought her back to life.

It wasn't Nick's kiss that had done it for Edie. It wasn't his lovemaking, either. It was simply him—his energy, his charm, his wit, his dazzling smile. And his eyes. His eyes were eloquent. They spoke to her without words. They laughed with her, they teased her. They bore witness to his suffering. They anguished with her about her own. They drew her in.

They woke her up.

The kisses, the lovemaking grew out of that. She thought maybe she'd gone to bed with him out of gratitude for her awakening. She was grateful. But it was more than that.

She'd felt a connection she couldn't explain—as if he'd given her something that night and, in their lovemaking, she had given him something in return.

She'd tried over the past couple of months to articulate what. She hadn't been able to. Not really. If he'd come after her, she might have been able to. But of course he hadn't.

It had been a one-off, just as he'd said it would be.

So what was he doing here now?

His mobile mouth tilted into a conspiratorial smile and his eyes—those dark, sometimes laughing, sometimes brooding eyes—were just as intent as ever as they focused on her.

Once more Edie felt the connection she'd felt that night in Mont Chamion.

So whatever it was, it had lasted—for her at least—longer than one night. Edie felt her breath catch.

"What— What are you doing here?"

The Cinderella inside her wanted him to say he was here for her. The other sane sensible 99.9 percent of her brain told herself to get a grip. Things like that didn't happen in real life. She wouldn't want them to happen!

"Nice to see you, too," Nick said amiably. Then he cocked his head and looked quizzically at her. "I don't remember us parting on bad terms. Actually I don't remember us parting at all. I woke up and you were gone." Now his eyes accused her.

Edie felt her face warm, her fingers tightened on Roy's collar. "You were asleep. I had a plane to catch." She tried to sound matter-of-fact. In fact she knew she just sounded defensive. "Sorry," she said after a moment. "It was…" She hesitated, trying to find the right word. "It was a lovely night."

That was inadequate. But what else could she say? And the situation wasn't one she'd ever been in before—or since.

He was still smiling at her, every bit as gorgeous as he had been that night, only this time in an easy California casual way. This Nick wore a pair of jeans, faded nearly white at the knees and thighs, a long sleeve sage-green oxford cloth shirt with the cuffs rolled half up his forearms and a pair of aviator sunglasses parked atop his midnight-black, wind-ruffled hair.

"It was," Nick agreed. His gaze moved over her slowly, as if he were undressing her again now. Edie felt her whole body warm.

And then he said, "I've been talking with your mother."

"My mother?" He was undressing her with his eyes and he'd been talking to her mother? Dear God, what had Mona done now?

"We were talking about an old adobe ranch house she's got."

Edie stared at him, feeling a total disconnect. "What?"

"She mentioned it when I met her in Mont Chamion," Nick went on. "She said it was in need of work. So I told her I'd give her an evaluation." He gave Edie an encouraging smile.

"Evaluation?" Edie echoed. He was here because he'd talked to her mother? It was business. It had nothing to do with her. She felt oddly deflated and off-kilter. She didn't know quite what to say, but Nick was watching her, clearly waiting for her to say something.

Finally she said the only thing she could think of. "Mona's not here. She's in Thailand."

"I know. I talked to her yesterday."

"Really?" Edie had talked to her mother yesterday as well, and Mona hadn't said a single word! The name *Nick Savas* hadn't crossed her lips. Nor had any mention of the adobe.

"We discussed renovations a couple of weeks ago," Nick said. "But I didn't know when I was going to be finished then. She said it didn't matter, just to come on ahead whenever I got my last job done." Nick spread his hands.

Pennies were slowly beginning to drop.

"Come ahead?" Edie echoed again, wondering if he thought it was strange that she couldn't seem to form a thought he hadn't already said. "For what?"

"The evaluation. Working on the house, if it warrants it." He reached out a hand to the dog, letting Roy sniff to make sure he was a friend.

Edie wished that was all the assurance it took. She felt pole-axed. And betrayed. Obviously when dangling Kyle in front of her didn't tempt Edie, she'd moved on to the man Edie had gone off with the night of the wedding.

Had she tracked Nick down and called him? Twisted his arm?

Edie was mortified beyond belief.

"You won't want to bother with the adobe," she said shortly now. "It's not worth saving."

That wasn't true, of course. Or at least she hoped it wasn't. She loved the old house where she'd lived as a small child. But that didn't mean she wanted her mother to hire Nick Savas to restore it!

Unfortunately Roy seemed to have accepted him as a friend. He began to slowly wag his tail. Edie anchored him firmly with a hand on his collar. She ground her teeth, trying to keep a polite smile in place.

"She made it sound as if it had possibilities," Nick said. "We won't know until I look at it, though," he added, as if to mollify her. "When I have, I told her I'd have a look and give her a call and talk to her about it. If it looks like a go, I'll do up a plan and explanations, then submit it for approval. There may be historical commissions to talk to, people to get on board. We'll cross those bridges as we come to them." This was Nick the professional talking, detailing all the steps with easy confidence.

Edie barely heard them beyond registering that all these bridges he was going to have to cross would take time. And time meant—

"Where are you staying?" she asked abruptly.

Nick blinked, then the lopsided smile reappeared. "Well, Mona invited me to stay here."

Edie felt as if she'd been punched in the gut.

"Is that a problem?" Nick asked. He was looking at her speculatively.

"I—" Edie managed one word, then her speech dried up.

Problem wasn't precisely the word. Try *awkward,* she thought. Try *disconcerting.* Or *mortifying.* But how could she explain? She'd told him that Mona was matchmaking back in Mont Chamion. She didn't want to have to admit it again. She didn't want him to think her mother was trying to serve him up on a plate!

Deliberately she pasted on her best *mi casa es su casa* smile. "Of course not," Edie lied and stepped back to open the door wider. "Not a problem. I was just surprised. Come in. This is Roy, by the way."

Nick hunkered down and ruffled Roy's ears. The dog, a

sucker for ear rubs, moaned his pleasure. The sound made Edie remember all too well how Nick's hands had made her moan, too.

She was sure her cheeks were flaming when he gave Roy's ears one last rub, then stood up. "I'll just get my bag from the car."

Edie waited by the door and tried to gather her wits, to find a proper emotional leg to stand on from which to handle the sudden appearance of Nick Savas into her life.

He wasn't here for her, she reminded herself. At least not in his estimation. He'd come because her mother had given him some song-and-dance about renovating the adobe. And he didn't care enough about her one way or the other to let it sway him.

"It's business," she told herself firmly. "Remember that," she muttered under her breath as he strode back up the driveway with a leather and canvas duffel in one hand and a battered laptop case in the other.

"What's that?" he asked, obviously having heard her saying something.

Edie shook her head. "Just talking to myself. I need to remember something."

"You should write it down."

Yes, Edie thought. *I should. I should emblazon it on the insides of my eyelids.*

"I'll do that," she told him briskly, then took a deep breath and turned to lead him back into the house. "Right this way."

"Amazing place," Nick said appreciatively as he followed her.

The living room, with its high ceilings, thick cream colored rough plastered walls and terrazzo floors, opened through a series of French doors onto a broad patio with a trellised canopy sheltering it from the sun. The doors at this time of year were open, and the light afternoon breeze drifted in, stirring a set of shell wind chimes as they passed.

"It's hardly authentic," Edie said over her shoulder, glad that he was looking around rather than at her. "It's what my brother calls 'Movie star Spanish.'"

Nick laughed. "I recognize it." Then he shrugged. "But it pays homage to the real thing in an impressive way. The purists hate it, but it celebrated the heritage and the history in its own way. It's made it popular and accessible."

"You're more forgiving than my brother." Edie was surprised at his attitude. She would have thought an architect, especially one who dealt with authentic historic preservation and restoration, would be more judgmental, not less.

"It is what it is," Nick said, running his hand up the smooth dark bannister as she led him up the broad staircase, then looked back at the room below them. "A romantic idealization. It's not pretending to be authentic. Maybe your brother is responding not to the house but to what it means to him."

Which was probably truer than he could know, Edie thought. And Ronan wouldn't like being called on it, either.

"You could be right," she said as they reached the open hallway on the upper floor.

"You can pretty much have any of these that you want." She gestured at the several open doors. She showed him all the ones that were available, at the same time pointing out her mother's suite at the far end of the hall, then her youngest sister, Grace's, room and the twins' room overlooking the pool. "They're in Thailand with Mona right now," she said. "For the summer holidays."

She used to do that herself when she was young, trail after her mother and watch the filming from the sidelines. Those experiences had made her certain she never wanted to do what her mother did, at the same time it had made Rhiannon long to get in front of the cameras.

"How about this one?" Nick said, looking into a spare masculine looking room. It was almost Spartan in its lack of decor.

"Ronan, my older brother, uses this one when he's here. But

he won't be here for months, so you're welcome to it. Or," she added with a grin, "you can have the tower room."

"Tower?"

"Surely you noticed our pseudo-Moorish tower when you drove up." It was the most romantic of all the romantic elements in the house.

He grinned. "I'd forgotten that. There's a bedroom up there?"

"A small suite. Rhiannon loves it." She pointed at the narrow staircase that curved upward.

"Why am I not surprised? Does she use it when she's here?"

"Yes. But she's gone right now. You're welcome to it."

"I'd have thought you'd have first dibs on it."

"Never wanted it."

He raised a brow. "Not a romantic?"

"No." Not about rooms, anyway. And she tried to be realistic. At least most of the time. "That was my room." She tilted her head toward one that looked up toward the woods.

"Was? Which one is yours now?"

"I have an apartment over the carriage house."

It was a small, cozy one-bedroom flat that had been the caretaker's place when Edie was growing up. But then the caretaker left, and Ronan had taken over the carriage house during college. He'd kept it even after he got his first job as a journalist. But eventually he was out of the country so much he decided he didn't need it.

Edie had moved in there when she came back after Ben had died. She would work for her mother willingly, but she wasn't going to live with her, too. She'd been a married woman, Now she was a widow. She wanted her independence.

For all the good it was obviously doing her!

"So who's sleeping in your bed?" Nick asked.

Edie opened her mouth and promptly shut it again, face burning. Then she realized he meant the bed in the room that had been hers. "No one," she said hastily, which was in fact the answer to who was sleeping with her in the carriage house, too. Not that he would care.

"Then I will," he said and walked in and dumped his duffel bag and laptop on the bed.

She wouldn't let herself read anything into his choice. It was a fine room, and there was nothing of hers left in it. At least she hoped there wasn't. Not that Nick Savas would care if there was. To him it was a place to sleep.

"Great," she said with all the brisk indifference she could muster. "Well, I'll just leave you to get settled in."

"Who else is here?" he asked.

"Just you. But don't worry. Clara—she works for Mona, cleaning and sometimes cooking—will come in and cook for you. She lives in Santa Barbara, but she comes up every day and cooks for the family when Mona and the kids are home. She regularly does it for guests, too."

Nick shook his head. "Not necessary. I can cook for myself. Besides," he reminded her, "I might not be staying. Gotta see if it's worth it."

"Of course."

He might be gone before nightfall. Life would go back to normal. Edie crossed her fingers.

"Do you want to take a look at the old house today, then? Or are you tired from traveling?"

"I'm fine. Just flew up from L.A. I was visiting my cousin."

"Demetrios?" She knew he and Anny kept a place there for when his work took him to Hollywood.

But Nick shook his head. "Yiannis."

If Edie remembered right from the wedding, he was Demetrios's youngest brother. Another lean, dark, handsome Savas male. "Is he an actor, too?"

Nick laughed. "You wouldn't catch him dead acting. He works with wood. Makes furniture. Imports and exports everything from raw lumber to finished pieces. He's done some pieces for restorations I've worked on. Talented guy."

"Apparently." Edie smiled and began to back toward the door. "Come down when you're ready and I'll take you to see the adobe. I'll be in my office. It's in the back of the house, beyond the kitchen. If you get lost, follow the sound of the phone."

It was ringing now. And so she had the excuse to dart off to answer it. She gave him a quick smile and a little waggle of her fingers, then hurried back down the stairs.

It was the first time in weeks she was glad to hear Rhiannon's voice when she picked up the phone. Even when her sister said, "I've changed my mind," Edie didn't snap.

She just grabbed a pencil and said, "Okay. Tell me what the new plan is."

If Rhiannon noticed that Edie wasn't peevish, she didn't remark on it. But then she rarely seemed to pick up on other peoples' reactions. Now she just began explaining her most recently changed decision, which was to go meet Andrew in Miami next weekend instead of following up on meeting with a director about a film set in Turkey.

"So you can change it, right?" Ree demanded.

"I can change it," Edie assured her. It just meant starting over from scratch, canceling the reservation she'd made an hour ago. But at least she'd have something to occupy her mind that she could handle—unlike the man upstairs.

No, she told herself firmly. She could handle him, too. She just needed a little space and a little time to regroup.

She was just surprised, that's all. She hadn't expected to see him again. She might have hoped, yes—just a little—but she hadn't really considered it. And then when he did turn up, she'd dared to believe he had come to find her, to explore the connection she had sensed between them.

And then she'd discovered he'd come because her mother had asked him to—on the flimsiest of pretexts!

"Edie! Are you there?" Rhiannon's voice broke into her mental conundrum.

"Of course I'm here. Did you think I'd hung up on you?"

"You're not talking." It sounded like an accusation.

"I'm writing down the information you just gave me," Edie said. It wasn't totally a lie. She'd made a couple of notes. "I'll make the reservations now. I'll send you an email and forward them."

"Great. Thanks. You're the best. Don't tell Andrew," Rhiannon added quickly. "I want to surprise him."

"Are you sure?" Surprises were sometimes not the best idea.

"I need to make a gesture. To show up when he's not expecting me, when he's given up all hope!"

Ah, the drama of it.

"Whatever," Edie said vaguely.

"Thanks, Ede. Love you!" Rhiannon trilled and rang off, leaving Edie to muster her wits and check her watch. It was the middle of the night in Thailand or Mona would be getting an earful.

The phone rang again, distracting her. And two more calls after that forced her mind back to her work so that she actually jumped when a voice behind her said, "So this is where you work."

She spun around to see Nick standing in the doorway, hands braced on the uprights as he looked around and then let his gaze come to rest on her. There was a smile on his face.

Business, Edie reminded herself sharply. *Just business.*

"This is my office," she agreed with a sweep of her hand taking in the room. Mona called it "command central" but it really looked more like a comfortable den than anything else. There was a wall of bookshelves on either side of the fireplace, wide planked floors with a deep burgundy and navy blue Turkish rug, a pair of upholstered armchairs, a comfortably saggy sofa, a double-length heavy Spanish style oak desk with Edie's computer, printer, scanner and a stack of in-and-out boxes without which she would not be able to survive.

But most impressive of all was the view.

One wall was mostly glass, comprised of floor-to-ceiling

windows around the Spanish-style equivalent of French doors, which opened onto a terrazzo-tiled ramada overhung with bougainvillea. It looked out onto a broad rolling expanse of lawn with an inset naturally landscaped nearly Olympic-size swimming pool. Below the sweep of lawn and the pool, the land fell away steeply so that a grove of eucalyptus treetops were at eye level. Beyond them you could see the rooftops of Santa Barbara and, in the distance, the bulky shape of the Channel Islands in the sea.

"Not bad," Nick murmured, taking it all in. He slanted her an amused glance. "I'm surprised you get any work done."

"You get used to it," Edie confessed as she stood up. "It seems a sacrilege to say so, but unless I consciously stop and look—and sometimes I do—most days I don't see it. I see work."

Nick nodded. "Understandable. It's the same when I'm working on a building. It's usually some massively impressive place in all the guide books, and all I see is rising damp and rotting timbers."

"Were there rotting timbers in the stave church?" she asked him. When he'd given her his "tour" in Mont Chamion he had mentioned that his next project was to be a Norwegian stave church restoration. Edie hadn't been familiar with stave churches then, but as soon as she got home, she'd looked them up online. Now she knew they were medieval wooden churches, and she could well imagine they'd have a few rotten timbers after all these years.

"There were." Nick nodded. And then he did what she hoped he would do—he began talking about the project.

As long as he kept talking about the church, she could focus on that. She could remind herself that he was here on business, and that it had nothing to do with her.

But then, on the way out of the house, she grabbed a baseball cap and yanked it on. In the summer Santa Barbara, particularly away from the ocean's edge, could be hot in midafternoon. Once the sun broke through the fog that usually blanketed the coastline until late morning, it beat down relentlessly. And while inside fans were enough to keep things cool, outside Edie regularly wore dark glasses and an old baseball cap of Ronan's to shade her eyes.

"Very fetching," Nick drawled, a corner of his mouth tipping in a grin as he studied her. Then he reached out and tugged the bill of the cap.

And suddenly remembering this was just business wasn't so easy.

"I sunburn," she said, trying to sound matter-of-fact. Then she headed out the door. "This way."

She headed across the driveway and up the path past the carriage house. The groomed lawns didn't extend to this side of the property. It was brush and chaparral and eucalyptus, with a sort of vague path through it that led up the hill. Roy ambled on ahead, nosing in the under brush.

"No road?" Nick said, striding alongside her, easily keeping pace.

"There's a rough one," Edie told him. "But it doesn't come past the house. It goes around the side of the hill and winds a bit. So it's generally faster to walk—unless you'd rather not."

His hair was ruffled and damp on his tanned forehead and she thought he did look a bit tired. But he just laughed. "Is that a challenge, Miz Daley?"

Something in his drawl made Edie's skin prickle with awareness. It was perverse, really. For two and a half years after Ben died, she felt no interest, no awareness of the opposite sex at all. Then, that night in Mont Chamion, the very sight of Nick Savas across the ballroom with her sister, had jolted her awake. His appeal as the night went on hadn't lessened, and it had certainly taken her mind off thoughts of Kyle Robbins. Still, she'd expected that, not seeing him again, her reawakened hormones would have noticed another man in the meantime.

But they'd gone right back to sleep—until now.

Now she tried to ignore them as best she could. "Just asking. We can drive if you want."

He shook his head. "I'm good," he told her and started walking again. "I was just wondering how I'd get materials to the house."

Right. Business.

So Edie pointed out where the road went as they climbed the hill. Once there had been a path through the woods that led from the new big house back to the old adobe. But in the past fifteen years or so, it had overgrown as the family had gone back there less and less.

It meant something to Ronan and Edie. But the rest of Mona's children had been raised in the new one, so they had no memories and little interest in a derelict run-down ranch. Even the twins, who thrived on the prospect of adventure, especially where mud and dirt were involved, had really never shown much interest in it. It wasn't exactly exciting, though Edie loved it.

Occasionally she had thought she would love to restore it and make it into the family house it had once been for them when she was a child. She hadn't said anything to Ben about it, though. There had been no point when they were in Fiji. And she'd always thought there would be time.

Now she was glad she hadn't. She had only come back a few times since his death—mostly to bring the twins and Grace to the house, to try to interest them in it, to tell them stories there and give them a sense of connection to a past they were only peripherally part of.

"I thought you didn't do houses," she said now as she and Nick made their way up the path.

"Maybe I won't," he said. "I have to see it first."

"Of course. It was nice of you to come all this way to look at it and give Mona an opinion," Edie said, striving to sound properly businesslike. "I don't know why she is so keen on doing it now."

Well, she did, actually. And it had nothing to do with the

house itself. But just how blatant had Mona been in her attempt at matchmaking? Edie slanted a glance at Nick as they walked, but he didn't reply, and the look on his face didn't give anything away.

"When did you finish at Mont Chamion?" she asked.

"I left a week or so after the wedding. There were some talented local craftsmen who continued the work while I was in Norway. I went back a couple of times to make sure everything was going well, but I've been in Norway and Scotland most of the past two months."

"Scotland?"

"Mmm. Tell me about the ranch house."

So much for getting him talking. But the ranch house was business, too, so Edie did as he asked.

"I think it's from the mid-nineteenth century. Pretty primitive to begin with, I think. My dad used to tell us stories about the ranchers who lived here. I don't know how true it was. Dad liked to tell stories." She smiled now as she remembered the delight Joe Tremayne had taken in gathering her and Ronan onto his lap and regaling them with tales of early California.

"Was it in his family?" Nick asked.

"No. My mom and dad bought it right after they married. It was pretty run-down already by then, but the land was what my dad wanted. He was raised on a ranch north of San Luis Obispo. His dad was a foreman there. Dad wanted to raise cutting horses. That was his dream. He dabbled in winemaking, too. He wasn't a Hollywood sort of guy." In her mind's eye she could still see her tall, handsome father with his shock of dark hair and wide mischievous grin. "He was a good balance to my mother. Solid. Dependable. Steady." She caught herself before she went any further. "But you don't care about that. You want to know about the house."

"I want to know it all," Nick said, his eyes on hers. "About the house, of course. But it's important to understand the people who live—or lived—in it. What mattered to them. What they valued."

Edie thought about that. She remembered him telling her about the history of the castle at Mont Chamion and about the royal family there. She guessed it was the same here.

"Family," she said firmly. "That's what they both wanted. Even Mona," she said before he could raise his brows in doubt "My dad's death changed her. He was her anchor. When he died, it was like she'd been cut adrift. She was lost. She wanted what they'd had—what we'd all had—and she kept trying to get it back."

Telling him about it now, she could see it all again—the happy days they'd spend as a family in the old adobe followed by the painful dark days after the car accident that had taken her father's life. Her voice trailed off as they crested the hill and headed down the other side. The old house came into sight beyond a stand of eucalyptus.

"Hence the marriages?" Nick ventured.

"Pretty much," Edie agreed. "She wanted to be married. She wanted a man. And men want Mona. They always have. So they kept proposing, and she kept saying yes. And she kept having babies," she added a little wryly.

"That must have been difficult for you."

"No. It was great, especially after she got to be so famous. It was easier that there were six of us. It diluted the paparazzi's attention."

They were approaching the house now, and Edie was appalled at how run-down it looked. Tried to see it from Nick's perspective. She imagined he was mentally packing his bags, ready to declare it worthless. It certainly didn't look salvageable to her. And it had an empty forlorn air very much at odds with how she remembered it.

"It's a lot worse than I remembered," she said. "It wasn't like this when I was growing up here."

Nick didn't say anything. He just stopped on the slope and

studied the sprawling one-story adobe structure with its broad front porch and deep-set windows.

"It wasn't in the best shape when they bought it," Edie said quickly. "I remember Mona saying they got it cheap as a 'fixer-upper.' But my dad did a lot of work on it," she added defensively. "But he was busy making a go of the ranch and the horses. He didn't have a lot of time."

"Understood." Nick made his way down the rest of the dusty slope and began a closer inspection.

Edie, following him, recognized how very neglected the house had become. The broad front porch covering sagged. Pieces of the *zaguán* were broken or altogether missing. Places that her father had tried to patch with stucco had crumbled away and the adobe beneath them was crumbling as well.

Nick took his time, walking around the building slowly, looking at it from all angles while Edie followed, looking at the house, but also at him. He moved with the easy grace of some sort of jungle cat. Last year when she'd taken Ruud and Dirk to the San Diego Zoo, she'd been fascinated with the grace of a tiger moving through the brush. She thought of that tiger now as she watched Nick prowl around the house. He took hold of one of the timbers that poked out from the roof and jerked it. The crack of the wood made Edie wince.

"Probably not worth restoring," she ventured.

He didn't reply, just kept moving. He paused to pick at some of the stucco her father had used to repair part of the crumbling back wall, then watched it flake and fall to the ground. Another reason to wince.

It was good, she tried to tell herself. With all these things wrong with the house, the less likely he was to stay and Mona's heavy-handed efforts at matchmaking would come to naught. But at the same time she didn't want the house to fall down. And the Cinderella gene she was trying to ignore still wanted Nick Savas to stay.

"Is it unlocked?"

So the outside hadn't totally discouraged him?

"I have a key." She dug into her pocket and pulled out a set of keys, then chose the one to open the front door. Nick took it wordlessly from her. Their fingers brushed. Yes, heaven help her, even with a simple touch the awareness was still there.

In one long leap Nick vaulted onto the porch and opened the door.

Edie followed him more carefully, picking her way past the broken wooden steps up to the porch. "The electricity's off," she said. "I'm afraid you can't see much."

With a forest of towering eucalyptus all around, the house never received the brunt of the direct sun. It was far cooler that way, but the interior, shrouded in shadow and with only very deep-set windows, was barely visible when Edie followed him in the front door.

Apparently Nick was used to doing things by feel. As she watched, he moved around the room, running his hands over the walls, peering up at the ceiling, crouching down and studying the floor.

Edie didn't know what he was seeing, but the longer she stood there, the more she saw memories of the house she'd been happy in as a child. This living room was the place where her dad had crawled around on the floor giving her horsey rides. Over by the window was where they'd put up the Christmas tree. In the big kitchen they had eaten meals her mother had actually cooked instead of those a cook made for them.

The memories made her throat ache as she looked around.

She walked around, touching things, recalling things. She ran her hand over the kitchen countertop and remembered standing on a chair helping her mother cut out cookies there. By the back door there were still the marks on the wall where her dad had marked her height and Ronan's every few months. How small she'd been.

She rubbed her thumb over the last, highest pencil mark and remembered how she used to stretch as tall as she could, and her dad would press his hand on the top of her head, laughing. "Stop that! You're growing too fast already!"

"You okay?" Nick appeared in the doorway, looking concerned.

Edie mustered a smile. "Just remembering." She gave the wall a little pat. "It's been a long time. This a good place. I was just remembering how good it was."

Nick nodded as if he understood.

Maybe he did. She didn't know that much about him. The trouble was, what she knew she liked. And seeing him here made things somehow even more difficult.

When she'd had one night with him in a completely foreign setting, it was easier to tell herself she wasn't really interested, that her awareness of him was a momentary aberration, that back in her own life, she wouldn't really notice.

But she did.

He was opening the cupboards now, peering inside. And she allowed herself to study him because he wasn't paying attention to her. She had run her fingers through that tousled hair. She'd nibbled her way along his stubbled jaw, then pulled off his tie and unbuttoned his shirt. Now, as he shut the cupboards and crouched down to look at the floor, she watched the muscles in his thighs bunch and flex beneath the worn denim covering his thighs and remembered that she had touched him there. And he had touched her, too.

Not just her body—but something fundamental deep inside her. Something that she hadn't managed to forget.

"I have to go," she said abruptly, her announcement rather louder than she intended. "I have work to do."

From where he was crouched on the floor studying the boards, Nick glanced up at her and nodded. "Yeah. Sure. Fine. Go ahead." He sounded as if he'd already dismissed her from his mind.

No doubt he had, Edie thought. She turned and hurried out

of the house. "Come on, Roy," she called to the dog who was nosing curiously around the edge of the porch.

Roy looked at her, then back at the house, as if he expected Nick to join them.

"He's not coming," Edie said, more for her own good than for the dog's. "He's here on business. And then he's leaving."

She hoped.

At least she thought that was what she hoped. He wasn't here for her. He had awakened her, but he didn't want her. He thought he was here for work, but it was really because Mona had been playing matchmaker again.

Edie glanced at her watch. It was early yet in Thailand, but so what?

If Mona thought she was going to get away with meddling in Edie's life, she deserved an early wake-up call!

He'd hadn't made any promises.

"I'll take a look at the adobe," Nick had told Mona on the phone last week. "You don't want to throw money down the drain. If it isn't a good candidate for restoration, I'll tell you."

"Fine. Good. Whatever you think," Mona had said. "You can stay at my place. There's plenty of room."

"I'll do that," he'd said. "But it might not be worth it."

"Understood." Mona had sounded impatient. "Got to go. We're shooting now. Discuss it with Edie. She can show you around. You remember Edie."

He remembered Edie.

She hadn't changed a bit.

Her utilitarian ponytail hardly recalled the sophisticated up-swept hairstyle she'd worn to the wedding. And her casual canvas pants and open-neck pink shirt might mask the curves the purple dress had highlighted.

But Nick was willing to bet that, unloosed, her hair would cascade down her back in those wondrously silken waves. Just as he knew damned well that underneath whatever Edie Daley wore, he would still find her petal-soft skin and the womanly secrets he'd only once had a chance to explore.

"Hell," he muttered, scowling toward the door she'd walked out of moments before.

Hell—because she was just as appealing as she had been back in Mont Chamion. He'd hoped she wouldn't be. That was why he'd been at pains to make sure Mona understood he might not stick around.

Maybe the house wouldn't be worth working on—or maybe he'd take one look at Edie Daley and decide that their one night in Mont Chamion was the extent of her appeal.

No such luck.

Now he stood in the shadows of the window and watched her until she was out of sight.

She was still wearing the baseball cap, with her hair pulled back into a ponytail and poking out through the space above the adjustable strap at the back of the hat. And she really didn't have any noticeable curves. In fact, from the back he was disconcerted to discover that she could probably pass for a tall, slender twelve-year-old girl.

So why, for two and a half months, had he not been able to get her out of his mind?

Nick had never dwelt on the women he bedded. Had no interest in them beyond the night they spent together. They were fun and attractive and he had a good time with them. But as soon as they were gone, he moved on and never looked back.

End of story.

He couldn't even have told you half their names. But he couldn't forget hers: Edie Daley.

Edie of the long dark curls and flashing green eyes, of the wide mobile mouth and the very kissable lips. Lithe and limber Edie. Eager and passionate Edie. Her spark, her charm, her curiosity, her vulnerability, all had haunted him every night, and plenty of days. Since he'd shared his bed with her.

Two and a half months and he hadn't been able to forget her. It was absurd.

At first Nick thought the memories kept coming back because they'd spent the night in *his* bed. He had always made a point of never sharing his own bed with a woman.

He didn't bring them onto his turf.

Hell, he didn't even have turf. He didn't own a house, didn't rent a flat. He had no place to call his own. He'd sold the house he'd built for Amy as soon as he could after her death. He wanted nothing more to do with it.

He left what little personal gear he didn't carry with him at his uncle Socrates's house on Long Island. And he stayed on the move, living in someone else's house while he renovated it. It suited him perfectly. He had no reason to have a house.

He had no wife. No kids. No dog nor cat. No encumbrances at all.

He didn't need them. Didn't want them.

And he didn't want Edie Daley, either!

Well, he did. Carnally, at least, Nick admitted, he wanted her a hell of a lot. But that was all.

The desire was an itch he needed to scratch. So, he'd scratch it and it would be gone, and that would be that.

CHAPTER FIVE

"WHAT do you mean she's gone?" Edie demanded.

The Thai woman on the other end of the phone connection didn't speak particularly good English, which gave Edie hope that she might have heard wrong. But when the woman repeated her words, the meaning was the same the second time around.

"Miz Tremayne go away for work. Not here."

"But it's barely light," Edie protested. "What on earth time did she go?"

"She go last night."

"Last night? But she didn't mention anything yesterday."

"Change of plan," the woman said. She didn't sound as if it was any big deal. Probably for her it wasn't.

"When's she coming back?"

"Don't know. Three, four, five days maybe. They go to mountains."

"Mountains?" That didn't sound good. And they were going to be gone days? "But I need to talk to her."

She was only calling the phone at the house Mona had rented because she had already tried Mona's mobile phone half a dozen times. Each time it had gone directly to voice mail.

At first she'd thought her mother was simply avoiding her. But after two hours with no reply, she knew something else was going on. Mona was a stickler for returning messages. The only time she didn't call back was when she was in the middle of a scene or completely out of range.

Obviously now she was out of range. But for *days?*

"Where are the kids?" Edie asked. Ordinarily her mother would have sent for her to take care of them while she was gone. Surely she hadn't just left them with the woman who cared for the house.

"They go, too."

"Ah. Well, um, good." At least Edie hoped that was good. There was no doubt that Mona loved her children. But she also had a career that demanded she put it first most of the time. Taking the twins and Grace with her this summer—without having Edie along to keep an eye on things—was something of a first.

"Did she even take her phone?"

"She take it," the woman said. "But hard to get calls. You try," she suggested cheerfully. "Maybe you be lucky."

Luck, Edie could have told her mother's housekeeper, was not on her side at the moment.

She thanked the woman, tried Mona's number twice more, then gave up. There was no point in filling her mother's in-box with messages she wouldn't see until she got back to civilization. Besides, when she confronted Mona about her matchmaking, she intended to do it live and, if not face-to-face, then at least ear to ear.

She'd given Mona a piece of her mind after the Kyle Robbins incident at the wedding. She thought Mona had learned her lesson. Apparently not.

Still grumbling, Edie stared at the computer screen and tried to focus on the rest of the afternoon's work. She had phone calls to return, some correspondence from Mona's contracts lawyer to deal with and Rhiannon's plane reservations to cancel and rebook. Surely she had plenty to keep her busy—enough so that she wouldn't spend the rest of the afternoon thinking about Nick Savas.

Easier said than done. She got the reservations rebooked. She looked up the answers to the questions Mona's contracts lawyer wanted. She returned that call and several others. But all the while she did so, she had one ear cocked toward the door, expecting to hear it open, expecting the sound of footfalls heading toward the office.

Time passed. An hour. Two. By five-thirty he still hadn't come. Perhaps he'd taken a look around, then simply left. When she closed up the office she actually walked out to the front room to look out the window to see if his car was still there.

Of course it was. He couldn't have left without her knowing because he'd have had to come back for his bag. He'd already taken his duffel upstairs.

So did he expect her to simply sit in her office and wait for him?

Probably not, Edie admitted to herself. Probably he hadn't given her a thought at all.

"And you should stop thinking about him," she counseled herself.

So she did what she always did after work. She changed into her bathing suit, went out to the pool and dived in.

It was just past six when Nick got back to Mona's house.

He had gone over every inch of the adobe, had walked around kicking the foundation, prying up floorboards, clambering onto the roof. He was grimy, filthy, sweaty and hot and he needed a shower. Bad.

Now he went around the house to go through the doors closest to the stairs so he wouldn't track in dirt and dust. And so he could stop by Edie's office. But before he got there, out of the corner of his eye he saw movement that caught his attention.

Beyond the bank of oleanders growing partway down the lawn, someone was in the pool.

Before his brain made a conscious decision, his feet were already heading across the lawn toward where Edie's lithe form cut through the water as she did laps. Her stroke was smooth and even, but it wasn't her stroke Nick was focused on. It was her body, her mile-long legs, her tanned back—all that lovely golden skin he remembered so well.

If he'd needed a shower before, he needed one worse now. A long icy cold one.

Or, he thought, he could dive into the pool, take Edie into his arms and solve all his problems at once.

Not a difficult choice.

He had unbuttoned his shirt by the time he reached the terrazzo-tiled patio where the pool was. He opened the gate, tossed the shirt onto a chaise longue and was toeing off his shoes and tugging his undershirt over his head at the same time.

"You're back." Edie's voice startled him.

Nick jerked the T-shirt the rest of the way off to see her, out of the pool now, coming toward him. She had a towel wrapped around her waist and she was rubbing her hair dry with another. He couldn't see her legs anymore, but her bare midriff was enticement enough. As Nick watched, half a dozen droplets of water slid down her abdomen from beneath the top of her bathing suit.

He swallowed, staring as the drops disappeared into the towel knotted at her waist.

"So what do you think?"

"Think?" He wasn't thinking. Not with his brain anyway.

"About what?" he asked dazedly. She had to have seen him coming. Why the hell hadn't she stayed in the pool? Was she trying to avoid him? he wondered, nettled.

"About the house." She lowered the towel from her hair and peered at him over the top of it "Time to raze it? Cut our losses?" She sounded almost hopeful.

Was she hoping? Surely not. He'd seen the wistful look on her face this afternoon. He'd watched her move from room to room, running her hands over the woodwork and the cabinets, touching those little pencil marks by the back door.

"No," he said sharply, with more force than he intended. He moderated his tone. "No. It's quite salvageable."

"Really? And it should be?" Now she sounded surprised.

"It's an interesting piece of vernacular architecture," he said firmly. "Not all of a piece, of course. And not of huge historical significance," he added honestly. "But the fact that it's not a mansion, but a surviving example of small ranch architecture makes it worth restoring."

Also true. To a point. From a purely historical significance standpoint, the old adobe ranch house was such a pastiche of different styles, periods, restorations, disastrous additions and bad workmanship that, as a bonafide professional historical restoration expert called on to choose which buildings were worth preserving and restoring, he ought to have been running in the other direction.

But he wasn't.

He was standing here saying, "It can be salvaged," with an absolutely straight face.

And he was rewarded by seeing her face light up. "I thought you'd say it wasn't worth the trouble."

It wasn't. At least not solely on an architectural basis. But there were other reasons to restore things.

"It's worth it," he said.

She gave him an instant brilliant smile. But it faded quickly. "So what does that mean?" she asked, sounding almost wary now.

We make love right here on the chaise. Of course he didn't say that. He cleared his throat. "I put together a plan, talk it over with Mona, then get to work."

"So, you're…going to be staying a while?" She didn't sound thrilled.

"Yes," he said firmly.

Now she smiled again, but it still didn't seem to reach her eyes. "Well, um, great. That's just great."

"You don't want the house salvaged?"

Something flickered in her eyes. "No, I do. It's—" she hesitated, then the smile appeared again "—it's lovely."

"Then why don't I take you to dinner and we can celebrate?"

Edie blinked. She opened her mouth. But then she just stood there looking at him. No sound came out.

"Edie?" he prompted when seconds went by and she didn't speak.

"Celebrate?" she echoed at last.

"Sure. We have a lot to celebrate. That the house is worth fixing. That I'm going to be here a while. That we're both here," he added pointedly and turned the full heat of his gaze on her. "I think that's worth celebrating, don't you?"

He saw her swallow. Then she bobbed her head a little jerkily and took a breath. "Yes. Of course." Another breath, a brittle smile. "That would be nice."

"Nice?" He cocked his head, regarding her from beneath hooded lids. "Nice?" he repeated, teasingly.

Edie shrugged awkwardly. Her smile stayed in place but it looked even more superficial. Nick was reminded of the smile she'd worn when she'd reappeared at his side at the reception, when she had taken him up on his offer of a tour of his renovations. There had been a tense edginess about her then, too.

Then she'd been avoiding the hundred-dollar-haircut man and her mother's expectations. Was she nervous now? Uncertain? Wishing she could avoid him?

Nick scowled. Why would she feel that way? Didn't she remember how good it had been between them? If she didn't, he'd be happy to remind her.

"I need to get dressed," she said now, and she began edging toward the gate.

"Not on my account." He grinned.

A blush suffused every bit of Edie's visible skin, telling him that she certainly hadn't forgotten.

Even so, the look she gave him was pained. "If we're going out to dinner, I need to shower and wash my hair."

"We could get take-out, stay in, celebrate here." He could

think of excellent ways to celebrate that wouldn't require her dressing at all.

Edie shook her head. "No. If we're going to stay here," she said, "I have work to do."

"Then we're going out."

"But—"

"Go take your shower and wash your hair, Edie Daley. Get dressed if you must," he said. "I'll swim and change and be at your place in an hour."

All evening long it felt like a date.

Edie knew better, of course. Her mother had engineered the whole thing. But, knowing it didn't entirely save her. The minute she had opened the door to Nick standing on her small front porch, it felt as if he were courting her.

Wishful thinking, she'd chastised herself even as she let him open the door of his car for her and, for a moment, brush his fingers over hers as she got in.

Though her fingers tingled with awareness, Edie tried to keep things pleasant and businesslike. That's what it was, after all.

Business. It was like a mantra. She needed to keep the word going over and over in her head all the time—because the way he smiled at her, the way his eyes seemed to heat when his gaze met hers, the way, every time he refilled her glass of wine and handed it back to her, their fingers touched—all of it made her want more than she knew was really there.

It was a beautiful, cloudless California evening with the lightest of breezes, perfect for sitting at a table outside. The ambiance was casual, the food was fantastic and Nick was charming and flirtatious. She was sure he was like that with every woman he ever met, but telling herself that didn't make her any less susceptible to him.

He was too easy to talk to, too gorgeous to look at. He answered her questions about the stave church in Norway and another project he was working on at a Scottish castle.

"And yet you came here?" she said. Mona's powers of persuasion were legendary, but Edie was still surprised Nick had agreed, especially since he had to know she'd be here—and he didn't "do" relationships.

Or did he? The thought was tantalizing.

He had awakened her, after all. Perhaps she had done the same for him.

Edie leaned in to study him more closely, as if an intent examination of his features would give her the answer to the question.

"I came here," Nick agreed. He lounged back in his chair and regarded her from beneath hooded lids.

"Why?"

He blinked, as if her blunt question surprised him. But then he shrugged easily. "It's what I do. And," he added, one corner of his mouth quirking, "I like a challenge."

And there it was again—the hum of awareness that seemed to arc between them.

Physical attraction? Oh, yes. Anything more? Edie couldn't tell.

The noise of the dinner hour had abated and, as other diners left, their table, which was at the far end of the patio of the downtown Santa Barbara restaurant, became more isolated and intimate.

"Cup of coffee?" Nick murmured. He was watching her from beneath slightly lowered lids. A smile played at the corners of his mouth. Edie had no trouble remembering the taste of that mouth and the way his lips had felt pressed against hers.

It was time to go. Edie knew it. But going meant confronting the awareness sooner rather than later. And she wasn't ready yet. She needed fortification. So she said yes to the cup of coffee. It was strong, black, a full-bodied Colombian roast. Meant to be savored. Meant, she suspected, to give her the stamina—and the caffeine—to stay up all night making love with him.

Which she would dearly love to do. Except…

She clutched the cup like a lifeline, stared into it, trying to find the words to say what she needed to say. Finally she lifted her gaze and met his. "We need to get something straight."

At her tone one of Nick's brows lifted. "Oh?"

She gave a jerky little dip of her head. Her fingers strangled the coffee mug as she plunged straight to the heart of the matter. "I'm not sleeping with you."

Now both of Nick's brows shot up. He sat up straighter, looking first surprised, then almost bemused. After a moment, he settled back in his chair and picked up his own cup, holding it easily. "Aren't you?" His tone betrayed only mild interest, making Edie feel like an idiot. But she'd already begun, so she forged ahead.

"No. And yes, I know, you haven't asked." There, she'd pointed out the obvious, too. "But since we did once—" she took a quick breath "—I thought the issue could come up again."

"It could," Nick agreed. His tone was still mild, but there was a hint of something else, something deeper, yet definitely suggestive that told her she hadn't entirely misread the situation.

She met his gaze head-on. "So I thought I should make it clear up-front that it's not going to happen."

For a long moment Nick didn't say anything, but his gaze never wavered. Then finally, after what seemed like an eon, but was probably less than half a minute, he asked, "Why not?"

Edie swallowed. Her mouth was dry and her palms were damp, and she was already regretting having opened her mouth. She didn't do confrontation. Ever. She was a negotiator, not a battler.

Now she said, "It isn't that I didn't enjoy it." Her gaze dropped. She couldn't look at him squarely now. "I did," she admitted. Her cheeks were on fire.

"I'm glad." Nick's tone was grave, but when she dared look up, Edie thought she saw his lips twitch.

"You're laughing at me."

He shook his head. "I'm not. I'm...baffled." He set down his cup and seemed to draw himself together. "I was under the impression that we had both enjoyed it."

"Yes, well, um," Edie said. "I'm glad you did, too. But that was it."

"It?"

"A one-off. You said so yourself."

She thought his jaw tightened fractionally, but in the shadows she couldn't be sure.

"It wasn't a hard and fast rule." His tone was gruff. "I don't turn into a pumpkin if I make love to a woman two times."

Edie's mouth curved into a reluctant smile. "I'm glad."

"Do you?" he challenged her.

Slowly she shook her head. "Not a pumpkin, no."

"Well, then?" he demanded. Their eyes met again. She didn't see anger in his, thank heavens. It was more curiosity.

"I could fall in love with you."

"What?" His cup hit the table with a decided *thump*. Then he went absolutely still. "In love with me?" He sounded at worst appalled, at best disbelieving.

Edie shrugged. Too late to turn back now. "After…after Ben died," she explained, "I felt like I'd died, too."

Nick nodded almost impatiently. "Yeah."

"Months passed. I wasn't interested in going out. I didn't care about dating again. I…wasn't interested in any man." She hesitated, then spelled it out. "Until you."

"You don't love me," he protested.

"I know that!" Edie said fiercely. "But I like you."

"Yeah, well, I like you, too," he said, frowning. "But I'm not falling in love with you!"

"Exactly," Edie said. "And if I am starting to feel things again, I don't want to fall for someone who isn't interested. I've already done that," she told him.

He scowled. "When?"

"I was eighteen. Young, foolish. I should have known better. You remember the actor with my mother at Mont Chamion?"

"Him?" Nick looked appalled.

"He was charming. We dated. It meant more to me than it did to him." She refused to go into all the bloody details. "It wasn't like that with Ben," she said. "So I know how it's supposed to be."

"You do, do you?" His dark eyes glittered with challenge.

But Edie had no doubts about that. She wrapped her fingers around the coffee mug and met his gaze squarely. "Yes."

Nick's mouth twisted. His fingers drummed lightly on the tabletop. With his other hand he carried his coffee cup to his lips, his eyes never leaving hers. He still didn't speak.

Neither did she. Just as well. She'd probably already said far too much.

The waiter came and refilled Nick's cup, but Edie put a hand over hers and shook her head with a smile. "I've had enough," she said. "I won't sleep if I drink anymore."

The waiter shot a conspiratorial male look in Nick's direction. "Sleep is overrated."

Nick made an inarticulate sound, then said harshly, "Could you bring the check, please."

Edie reached for her purse. "I'll get it."

Dark eyes flashed. "The hell you will."

"It's business," Edie protested. "My mother—"

"Your mother has nothing to do with this!" Nick pulled out his credit card and thrust it at the returning waiter before he could even reach the table.

"Really, Nick—"

"Stop arguing, Edie." His tone was flat and uncompromising. "And put your wallet away."

Reluctantly Edie put it away. "I don't expect—"

"You've already made what you expect and don't expect quite clear. Let me make something clear, too—when I invite a woman out to dinner, I expect to pay. Got it?"

"Got it," Edie muttered.

The waiter came back with the tab, which Nick scanned

quickly, nodded and signed, then tucked his card and the receipt back in his wallet.

"You can tax deduct it," Edie suggested.

Nick glared at her. Then he stood and came around the table to pull out her chair for her before she could push the chair back and get up herself. All very gentlemanly and polite. Just as if she couldn't hear him grinding his teeth.

"Thank you," she mumbled as she stood. "And thank you for dinner."

"My pleasure," he lied. It had to be a lie. The hum of awareness was still there, but so was a sizzle of annoyance.

Edie quickened her steps as they headed for the exit. But the toe of her sandal caught on a protruding chair leg. She stumbled. Nick's hand shot out to catch her arm and keep her from falling.

"Thank you," she said, breathless.

"No problem," he said, tersely.

The problem was that he didn't let go. He walked beside her as they headed toward the lot where he'd parked the car, his fingers stayed on her arm. Through the thin cotton of her dress, she could feel them as if there was no barrier at all between them.

Once in the car, she gave him directions on how to get out of Santa Barbara and back up into the hills to Mona's house. He'd found it himself during the day. She knew it wasn't as easy at night. He didn't argue. He didn't discuss. He didn't talk at all. He followed her instructions without comment.

He didn't speak again until he'd parked the car and they were climbing the steps to her apartment.

She would have protested that she didn't need to be escorted to the door, but there was an implacability about him now that made her hold her tongue. If he wanted to walk all the way up, so be it. He wasn't coming in.

The porch wasn't big. As she got out her key, he was close enough that she could smell the woodsy scent of his aftershave. He was close enough that if she turned, she could go up on her tiptoes and kiss his lips.

She didn't turn. In fact she was glad she managed to stick the key in the lock without fumbling as her hands were trembling slightly. Only when she had the key in the lock, did she look around. "Thank you for dinner," she said politely.

Nick grunted, his lips pressed in a thin line. So much for all that Savas charm.

She gave him a quick smile, pushed open the door and went in. Roy came bounding to meet her.

"Edie."

She caught Roy by the collar and looked back at Nick. "Yes?"

His dark eyes bored into hers. "It's not a given, you know."

It? "What's not?"

"That you'll fall in love. People *choose* whether or not to fall in love. It's always a choice."

"It's—"

"Always a choice," he repeated firmly, cutting her off. "You just need to choose not to."

Edie opened her mouth to protest, but even as she did so, she knew there was no point. If Nick believed that, they would have to agree to disagree. "Good night, Nick."

"Good night, Edie." His tone was ever so slightly mocking. A corner of his mouth lifted slightly. "Let me know when you change your mind."

In the morning, he was gone.

She wasn't surprised to look out the window and see that his car wasn't there. He'd obviously decided that if bedding her wasn't going to be a perk of Mona's renovation job, he didn't want to be bothered.

In some perverse way, Edie thought perhaps she should be flattered.

At least it meant he had enjoyed their night together in Mont Chamion. But of course it also meant that he saw her presence as nothing more than an opportunity for physical release.

Maybe not so flattering after all.

"So I'm glad I said what I did," she told Roy over her morning oatmeal.

The dog cocked his head and grinned at her, then looked hopefully at the toast she was buttering.

"You've had enough," she told him. "And I don't feed you from the table."

But try convincing Roy of that. He made a low whining sound and didn't budge or blink an eye as long as the oatmeal and toast lasted. Edie rolled her eyes at him.

He grinned happily, then ambled over to Mona's house with her when she went over at nine to start work. She knew what he was thinking: it was always possible she would stop for a snack midmorning. He wouldn't want to miss that.

There was no sign in the kitchen that Nick had eaten before he'd left. It was just the way she'd left it yesterday—as if he'd never been here, as if it had all been a dream.

It hadn't been a dream. Perhaps, though, Edie thought, it was a wake-up call.

Maybe Mona was right. Now that her hormones had been re-awakened, maybe it was time for her to stop sitting at home and waiting for the right man to appear in her life. After the disastrous end to her relationship with Kyle, she hadn't sat home and moped. She'd gone back to the university where, a few months later, she'd met Ben.

He'd been the right man, just as clearly as Kyle had been the wrong one.

Maybe, now it was time to do that again. She had loved Ben, but she didn't want to spend the rest of her life alone. Ben wouldn't have wanted her to. So if Nick Savas was the wrong man, it was up to her to find the right one.

He'd done her a favor.

She kept telling herself that.

She even acted on it. When Derek Saito, a local English teacher, called that morning to ask if Mona would come and talk to the drama class when school started, she didn't just take down the information and promise to check with Mona and call him back. She actually chatted with him.

Derek was Ronan's age. They'd been in the same class in school. They'd been surfing buddies and had played tennis together. He'd been Ben's friend, too. And she remembered well how kind he'd been to her after Ben's death. Now, after she caught him up on what Ronan was up to, he asked about her.

"I'm all right," she said. "Working hard."

"Too hard, I'd guess." Derek knew her well. "As usual."

Every other time Edie had disagreed. But today she said, "You could be right. I need to get out more."

There was a pause, as if Derek hadn't been expecting that. But then he said, "So, want to go out with me?" There was a quick pause, then he said, "I'm not hitting on you, Edie. Not yet," he qualified. "Ben was too good a friend. But there's a concert on campus Friday night. Old-timers. Couple of eighties rock groups. Pure nostalgia…if you're interested?"

It sounded like fun. And Derek was a friend. She doubted he'd ever be more than that, but why not go? What was there to stay home for?

"I'm interested," she said. "Yes."

"Great!" There was a sudden spike of enthusiasm in his voice. "Dinner first?"

"I could cook," Edie offered.

"No. We'll grab a burger or something. I'll pick you up at six."

"Shall I meet you at the restaurant? You wouldn't have to come all the way out here." Derek lived in town. The university was several miles on the other side.

"I'll pick you up. My pleasure," he said. "See you then."

But the moment Edie hung up, she sat there a moment thinking, *What have I done?*

"Nothing," she said out loud with all the firmness she could muster. "You're going out with a friend. You're getting a life. Mona will be proud," she added wryly.

Speaking of whom, she had a few words to say to her mother. So she picked up the phone again and tried to ring Mona. Again she got no answer.

She'd already tried twice this morning, right after she'd come into the office. There had been no answer then, either, so apparently Mona was still out of range.

She supposed Nick had sent her an email to say he had decided not to do the renovations. Serve her right, Edie thought, for all her meddling.

But a part of her felt a little bereft because the adobe wouldn't be salvaged. Going back over there with Nick had reminded her that once upon a time it had been a nice house, that she had made lots of good memories there. She had hoped to make more with Ben, though, to be honest she wasn't sure that ever would have happened. She'd thought that maybe when they'd come back from Fiji they could have fixed it up as a vacation house, even though they'd probably live elsewhere close to wherever Ben worked—somewhere right on the water.

Now none of it would happen.

Life was what happened when you were making other plans. She thought it was John Lennon who had said that. But Mona said it, too. Her mother was just a fount of wisdom these days, Edie thought grimly.

At least she had made a plan. She was going to a concert with Derek on Friday. And this afternoon she was going to finish doing the filing she'd intended to do yesterday when Nick Savas had been the "life" that had interrupted her plans.

The phone rang. Edie picked it up. "Edie Daley."

"Hey," a gruff masculine voice she hadn't expect to hear ever again said into her ear, "can you meet me at the adobe with your key? I've got tools and a truckload of roofing tiles to unload."

CHAPTER SIX

SHE was still an annoyingly attractive woman, even when she stood there, hands on her hips, watching him back a truck down to the adobe, with her mouth opening and closing like a fish.

Nick gave her a wave and a cheerful grin through the open window as he passed. "Thanks."

If she replied, he didn't hear her. He didn't see her mouth move, either, but he was focused on getting the truck as close to the house as he could. When he had, he flicked off the engine and hopped out.

Edie was still standing in the yard. "What are you doing?" she demanded as he walked toward her.

"Going to start with the roof. Figured while I was in town, I'd see if I could get what I needed." He shrugged and spread his hands. "I did."

He couldn't get all of the tiles he would need. But he got all they had at the moment with more on order. By the time they arrived he would be ready for them. In the meantime he had to finish pulling the rest of the old roof off.

"You left," Edie said.

"No. I went into town. Had to file permits, pick up materials." He gave her his best sunny smile.

She still had her hands on her hips. "I thought you'd changed your mind and gone."

He'd considered it. Half the night, which he'd spent either restlessly prowling the house or swimming laps in the damn pool to take the edge off his frustration, he'd thought about cutting his losses, packing his bags and hitting the road.

God knew he had plenty of other jobs he could be working on. He had commitments lined up for the next two years. He'd had to do some serious shuffling to fit Mona's little ranch house in.

Which was why he was staying, he told himself. He'd said he would. But in fact he hadn't told Mona yet. She was unreachable—off somewhere at the ends of the earth in Southeast Asia shooting a film. She wouldn't even know he'd changed his mind until he was gone.

But he didn't go—wasn't going—because of the expressions on Edie's face when she'd walked around the old adobe yesterday afternoon. He'd been examining the walls, the roof, the foundation. But even more, he'd been studying Edie.

Her face was such a mixture of wistfulness, yearning, happiness and sadness as she'd drifted through the rooms, run her fingers over the woodwork, stood staring out the windows, that he'd spent far less time going over the bones of the house and far more time watching her.

And last night after her "I'm not sleeping with you" announcement, after which he'd been ready to leave, he remembered the way she looked, and he couldn't go.

Instead he'd gone downstairs and wandered around Mona's house looking at all the photos on the piano, on the bookshelves, on the walls.

Mona had her share of fine paintings and prints by well-known and not-so-well-known artists. But by far the most numerous framed pieces were family photos. Not one of them was of Mona alone—they were all of her children, her spouses (Edie's dad and the exes, he gathered) or family group shots.

There were a lot of Edie.

In the kitchen there were magnetic snapshots on the refrigerator—of all the kids, but he only noticed Edie. In one she was playing in the pool, her head thrown back as she laughed. In another she had her arms looped over the shoulders of a pair of identical redheaded young boys. They were freckled and gangly, but they had Edie's eyes. In a third she was sitting on the patio with her arms around Roy. She was smiling, but the wistfulness was there in this one.

He found others as well. He looked at them all—Edie as a girl on a pony with a boy who had to be her older brother, Edie suited up to play volleyball at some high school, Edie and Rhiannon, Edie and another girl who was also probably a sister, more of Edie and the twins. Edie and a handsome young man with their arms around each other and expressions of pure delight on their faces. It had to be Edie and her husband.

He almost couldn't look at that one, knowing what he knew. He wondered that she could. But there were several, including a larger more formal portrait that must have been taken on their wedding day. It was in pride of place on the piano. She must see it every single day.

He hadn't looked at a photo of Amy in years.

The photos—and the memory of Edie's face that afternoon—made him stay. She wanted the house salvaged. He could give her that.

Besides, he wasn't a quitter.

If she thought she could just say no and make them both miserable—well, she was wrong. He'd leave when he was good and ready to leave, when he could turn his back and walk away, which he would.

Because, as he'd told her, love was a choice. And he'd done it once. He wasn't doing it again. Ever. But that didn't mean they couldn't enjoy their time together.

He started off-loading the tiles. "You could help," he suggested, slanting her a glance. "Or not."

Edie didn't move for a long moment, but then he heard her footsteps coming toward the truck. "Ten minutes," she said. "Then I have to get back to work."

* * *

He was *staying?*

Still poleaxed from his phone call, Edie stared after Nick as he carried an armful of tiles to a spot near the side of the house. She still felt as if the breath had been knocked right out of her. She was giddy and panicky and perversely elated. At the same time she was trying not to feel anything at all.

She knew what he was doing.

He was calling her bluff. He was going to make her prove she could resist him. She ground her teeth, glaring at his back. But then, having put down the tiles, he straightened and turned and looked right at her, and she felt the giddiness again, and hoped to goodness she could do what she'd told herself—and him—was necessary.

It *was* necessary!

She knew herself. She knew how invested she became in relationships. She knew the pain that her unrequited love for Kyle had caused her. Even having gone to bed with Nick once had undermined her ability to remain uninvolved. She had told herself she could—but in the end, she'd cared.

She hadn't fallen in love. But she hadn't been able to forget him, either.

Now once more she tried to imagine taking Nick to her bed for as long as he was here, then smiling and saying goodbye whenever the house was finished.

Or sooner.

There was no guarantee he wouldn't get bored with her much sooner than it took him to finish the house!

He could share a bed with her once more or five times more and then decide it was time to move on, find another woman. He wouldn't even have to flaunt her in front of Edie. He could simply find a new bedmate.

And she'd be left, gutted, heartbroken.

In the end Nick was right—it *was* simple.

But he was wrong, too. He might find it easy to choose where he loved. But could she?

Again the answer was simple: no.

So she turned her head, refused to let her gaze linger on his easy walk, his lean muscular body, his smile, the gleam in his eyes. She helped him move the tiles, and tried to think about something else.

And when they had the truck unloaded, she said, "Goodbye."

"Au revoir," Nick said cheerfully. "That means I'll see you again."

"I know what it means," Edie said shortly. She felt like saying, *Not if I see you first.* "Come, Roy."

But Roy, perversely, was too busy following Nick around, watching what he was doing, deftly catching the occasional treat Nick tossed his way.

"I saw that," Edie accused him. "Roy, come on!"

But Roy only had eyes for Nick.

"He's my friend," Nick told her, grinning.

"Because you're bribing him," Edie said indignantly.

"You haven't ever heard the old saying, 'The way to a dog's heart is through his stomach'?"

Edie shot him a glare to keep from laughing. "Fine. Keep him with you. Just don't overdo it," she said irritably. "And don't lose him."

"No fear. We'll both be back for dinner," Nick promised.

Edie grunted her lack of enthusiasm about that and started up the hill.

"I'll pick up a pizza," Nick called after her. "What kind do you like?"

She didn't answer that. "I'm going to be busy." Busy avoiding him.

But if Nick got the message, he ignored it. "See you later."

She tried to make sure that wouldn't happen. She finished up at work early. She swam her laps early, so she would be done before he got back. And she was in her apartment making a salad for dinner when she heard his car.

The only reason she looked out the window was to see that

Roy was with him. Once she saw the big black dog, she turned away. So she wasn't prepared for the knock on her door.

"We're back," Nick announced unnecessarily. He had a pizza box in one hand.

She didn't invite him in. Apparently she didn't need to. He came in just the way Roy did, without an invitation. Only while Roy went straight to the food dish, Nick paused to look around at the overstuffed sofa and chair, the craftsman style bookcases and the library table that doubled as her dining room table. He nodded his approval. "Nice place. Suits you." He spotted the cat on the windowsill. "Who's this?"

"Gerald," Edie told him. "What are you doing here? I didn't invite you," she said pointedly.

"No, I invited you," Nick agreed. "For pizza," he reminded her when she looked blank.

"I said I was busy."

He looked around at the evidence of her doing absolutely nothing other than tearing up some salad greens. "Yeah, I can tell."

Breath hissed through Edie's teeth. "I don't want to have dinner with you."

"Because you'll fall in love with me." He paused, then the grin flashed again. "Or am I making myself so obnoxious that you can't stand me?"

"Getting close," Edie said, determined not to smile.

Nick shrugged equably. "Well, if you don't want to share the pizza with me..." He waved the box close enough that she could smell sausage and other mouth-watering pizza sorts of smells as he moved toward the door. Edie's stomach growled.

"Oh, fine. Sit down," she snapped.

He beamed. "Will do. Gotta clean up a bit first. You take care of this while I grab a quick shower." He thrust the pizza box into her hands. "Don't eat it all before I get back." And he ran lightly back down her stairs and headed for Mona's house.

She put the pizza in the oven and turned the heat on low

to keep it warm. Then she finished making the salad, adding enough for him now, and set the table for two. Roy looked hopeful. Gerald came over to see if there was something for him. Edie fed them both.

Then she told them sternly, "That's all you get. No sitting around watching us, looking hopeful."

"No, that would be me."

She whipped around to see Nick standing in the doorway. He gave her what was undeniably a hopeful look, tempered with a grin, as his gaze slid over her, making her all too aware of what he was hoping for. Edie steeled her heart—and her hormones.

"Don't," she said firmly.

He shrugged. "Okay," he said easily, dropping the hopeful look and heading straight for the table with the same single-mindedness Roy and Gerald had shown. "Starving," he said as he put a piece of pizza on her plate and one on his. Then he dished her up some salad and took some for himself. "This looks great."

It did. And she was hungry. So she ate.

For the first few minutes there was silence as they were both focused on the meal. But eventually Edie had had enough to be far more aware of the man than of the meal he'd brought.

When he finished his fourth piece of pizza, he leaned back in his chair and sighed. "Ripping off a roof gives a guy an appetite."

She'd noticed that he'd already begun when he'd called her to bring the key. Now she reached over to the counter and plucked it up and held it out to him. "You'd better have this. Then you won't have to keep calling me."

His lips twisted, but he took the key and stuffed it into the pocket of the canvas shorts he was wearing. "Thanks."

Their gazes met again. His dark eyes regarded her warmly. A slight smile played across his lips. She abruptly got up and carried her plate to the sink. "Thank you for the pizza," she said, running water to wash the dishes.

"Thank you for the salad," he said equally politely. He came up behind her, set his plate on the counter. He was so near she could feel the heat of his body. She added dish soap to the water, then began putting the dishes in, all the while aware of him right behind her. And equally aware when he moved away.

She breathed again.

"I've got some planning to do," he said. "So I'll say good night."

She looked over her shoulder, surprised.

Nick shrugged. "Unless you have a better idea?" There was that hint of hope again.

Edie shook her head. "No. No. I—good night."

It was the right thing to do, she assured herself when the door closed behind him and she heard his feet going down the steps. It was safer—far far safer—this way.

Nick finished ripping the roof off the next morning. The following day he cleaned and sorted tiles. It had been a while since he'd worked on a roof like this one. Putting new and old tiles together was a tricky business. He wanted to take his time.

And he wanted Edie to come back.

She hadn't been here since the first day. He barely saw her except at dinner. Somehow they managed to eat that together every night. Either she cooked and apparently felt obligated to feed him—"Mona's hospitality is legendary," she said, making it clear the meals were an extension of it—or he went into town and picked up take-away.

But other than at dinner, he didn't see her. She didn't come around the adobe at all. Well, no, that wasn't true. She was certainly there in spirit—in his head—even if she didn't set foot in the place.

On Friday as he removed the last of the rotten front porch beams before he put the new one up this afternoon, he could look across the roof line and see the rusty swing set near the trees.

Edie hadn't gone near it when she'd shown him the house, but he knew she must have played there as a child.

It took no imagination to envision her swinging high, short legs pumping furiously, long dark hair streaming out behind. He smiled as he saw it in his mind's eye because he knew exactly what she'd looked like. The dark-haired little girl who had been Edie graced half a dozen pictures in the upstairs hall at Mona's place.

Later when he ate his lunch in the kitchen at the rickety table, he thought about her eating meals here with her family. It was intriguing to think of Mona Tremayne cooking in this kitchen, of her not as a megastar but as a young wife and mother.

But it was more intriguing to think about Edie as a child.

As the sun spilled through the dirty windows, making patterns on the dusty floor, Nick tried to imagine her playing there with her brother. He was sure she had. He'd seen the flickering expressions on her face when she'd brought him here. He wondered about those memories.

Ordinarily when he thought about the earlier occupants of a building he was restoring, they were distant historical figures. They weren't the woman he'd had pizza with on Tuesday and meat loaf with last night, the woman he'd made love with in Mont Chamion, the proper, tart-tongued woman who had melted in his arms, the woman he couldn't stop wanting to take back to his bed.

But when he studied the vertical row of little ink marks climbing the wall by the back door—dark blue Rs for her brother Ronan, and bright red Es for Edie—once again she became the little dark-haired girl she had been when she'd lived here. He bet she had stood tall while her father measured her.

If he shut his eyes he could see them now in his mind. There was a photo in the hall of Edie and her dad. She had been sitting on the adobe's front porch steps, snuggled close under her father's arm. She'd had her head turned so that, instead of staring into the camera, she was looking up at her father as if he regularly hung the moon just for her.

The memory made Nick smile until he realized that within a year of that photo, Joe Tremayne had been killed in an accident and Edie's life had irrevocably changed.

It was a wonder she wanted to come back here at all.

The noise of clicking on floorboards jolted him back to the present, and he turned to see Roy pattering in from the living room across the dusty floor. His mood lightened and he looked up, expecting—hoping—to see Edie at last.

But no one was there.

"Where is she?" Nick asked the dog.

Not surprisingly, Roy didn't answer. He was more interested in what remained of Nick's sandwich, and he whined hopefully. Nick gave the crusts to the dog, stood up and went outside to look for her. "Edie?"

But no one answered. He called her name again. Nothing. Except that Roy, having swallowed the crusts in one gulp, had come outside, too, and stood on the porch, wagging his tail.

"You didn't come without her, did you?"

But apparently he had. Hope faded. Nick sighed and rubbed the back of his neck, kneading taut cords of muscle. "Well," he said to the dog, "make yourself at home. I've got work to do."

If Mona ever got back to civilization, Edie thought irritably, she'd be amazed at all the work her business manager had accomplished while she had been out of touch.

Edie always worked hard. But working all day and a good part of the night, determinedly refusing to let herself think about Nick Savas, was having an extraordinary effect on her work output.

Even in the instances where, previously, there would be half a dozen phone calls waiting to be returned when she got to work in the morning because people all over the world were involved with Mona, now Edie almost always picked up the phone regardless of the time of night.

Why not?

She wasn't sleeping.

And talking about whatever they wanted to talk about was safer by far than lying in bed, tossing and turning and thinking about the man asleep in Mona's house—the man who could be in her bed if only she'd let him.

But she wouldn't let him. Couldn't.

But she thought about him. Couldn't help herself.

She looked forward to their dinners every evening. Couldn't seem to help that, either. She was eager to learn what he'd done on the house every day.

"You should come and see," he said each evening.

But she always declined. "I've got too much to do," she said. But she was curious.

So was he. While she asked about his work, every evening he asked questions about the years she'd lived there.

Which had been her bedroom? When had the swing set been set up? Whose birthday present had it been? How had they celebrated Christmas when they'd lived there?

At first Edie was reluctant to answer. For years she had bottled up the memories because it had seemed safer that way. But under Nick's gentle questioning, she found herself talking more, remembering more—and finding joy in the flood of memories she'd kept close to her heart.

Why hadn't she done it sooner?

Because talking about her father had always caused her mother pain. Ronan, too, shied away from discussing their father. But then Ronan shied away from talking about everything. And no one else shared those memories. No one ever asked about them. Not even Ben, she realized. He hadn't probed, didn't want to make her sad. And Ben had always been busy looking forward.

But Nick asked.

And Edie talked. When she protested that she was talking too much about herself, that it was his turn, he obliged with stories about his own childhood—about summers on Long Island—he and his brother Ari with their Savas cousins, especially Demetrios who was his age and George who was the same age as his brother Ari.

"We were wild and crazy kids," he told her. "If there was trouble to get into, we found it."

He told her stories that made her laugh and he showed her scars that made her wince. And she realized that not going to bed with Nick wasn't stopping her falling in love a little bit more every night they shared a meal.

Each evening the dinners lasted longer, and it was harder to pull herself away and say she needed to get back to work.

But she did. She had to. It was all she could do for self-preservation.

But by Friday she knew it was a very good thing she had agreed to go out with Derek that evening.

Midafternoon, after she'd taken four high-pressure phone calls in a row and spent another hour fruitlessly trying to contact Mona about a script, she decided to take a break, go back to her apartment and figure out what she was going to wear.

"Come on," she said, turning to look for the dog as she hung up the phone, frustrated at still not reaching Mona. "Let's get out of here."

And that was when she realized Roy wasn't there.

"Roy?"

She got up from her desk and went out to the kitchen. Sometimes on hot days he would go lie on the cool tiles there. But not today.

"Roy?"

She went back to the office, and pushed open the door to the patio and called his name again. Since she'd adopted him from a rescue organization shortly after she'd come back to the States following Ben's death, Roy had been her shadow.

If she was in the office, he was by her chair. If she was stretched out on a chaise beneath the *ramada* making notes on scripts, he was always there. If she was swimming laps, Roy was lying on the tiles, one eye open, watching her. If she was eating a salad for lunch, he was sprawled on the kitchen floor looking hopeful—though admittedly salads weren't his favorite meal.

She tried to remember the last time she'd seen him. It had been at lunch, she thought.

He hadn't been enthralled when she'd begun to tear up salad greens. Had he wandered back toward her office? He could push the door open to go outside, but he rarely did—only if Clara was there cleaning or if her grandkids had come and were swimming in the pool would he leave Edie's side.

Roy was a social animal. He liked to be with people, and Edie was the only one around.

Except...

"No," she said aloud. "Roy, you didn't."

And, truthfully, she didn't believe he had gone all the way to the adobe to see Nick. Why would he?

But if he wasn't there, where was he?

Had something happened to him?

Please God, no.

But even as she thought it, the words formed a knot in her gut, bringing back the memory of Ben's disappearance all over again.

Rationally she knew it wasn't the same, Roy was a dog in his own territory. Not a man in a small boat on a stormy sea. Roy was capable and competent. But bad things happened even to the capable and competent.

Ben had been both. And he'd been a skilled sailor besides. He'd simply been in the wrong place at the wrong time. In high school, Edie's friend, Kelly, had lost a dog to rattlesnake bites. It wasn't common, but it certainly happened. And without warning.

Edie knew there was nothing she could have done to save Ben. But if something had happened to Roy...

He wasn't by the pool. He hadn't gone to the cutting horse arena. He was nowhere in the house or the carriage house. There was no place else to go but the adobe. It was close to half a mile away. She couldn't believe he'd gone that far.

But she had to check. Maybe at least Nick had seen him.

"Roy!" she called his name over and over as she went.

The first response came when she was not quite at the top of the hill. She couldn't see the adobe yet. The voice that responded was loud enough for her to hear, but strained.

Just two words. "He's here."

"Oh, thank God," she said aloud as she hurried over the rise.

She was elated to see Roy standing in the yard in front of the house, tail wagging happily, and horrified to see Nick, shirtless, halfway up a ladder, a huge heavy beam on one shoulder as he tried to climb.

One end was already in place, which must have been a chore in itself. But the other needed to be lifted up and slotted into the opposite end of the porch.

Even as she watched, the ladder seemed to teeter.

"Wait!"

The second she shouted she thought she'd made a mistake, that she could startle him and he could drop it, could fall and have it come down on top of him.

Fortunately he didn't. He stopped, then turned his head to look up the hill toward her.

Edie was already scrambling and skidding down. Roy, enthused at the sight of her, began barking and frolicking in joy.

"No! Roy, stop!" She could just imagine him hurtling against the ladder and sending Nick flying.

For once in his life, Roy listened. He stopped at the bottom of the broken steps and squirmed, wagging his tail furiously as she reached the yard and glared up at the man on the ladder.

"What on earth are you doing? You could kill yourself!"

"I've done it before." His voice was still strained, undoubtedly from the load he was bearing.

Edie could see the sweat trickling down the side of his face and making paths through the dust on his shirtless back. "And lived to tell about it, apparently. But that doesn't make it sensible. You need help."

"You volunteering?"

"Yes, I am." And she brushed past Roy and took hold of the ladder, standing behind Nick, bracing her hands on the sides to keep it steady as he climbed.

Startled, Nick looked down at her. "Get out of there. You're right in the line of fire if I drop this thing."

"Then you'd better not drop it." She stayed right where she was, nose to the back of his denim-clad knees.

"Edie!"

"Nick!" she countered, still not moving.

"Damn it," he muttered under his breath. But when she still didn't move or relinquish her hold, she saw the legs of his jeans shift as he tensed his muscles and climbed another step. The ladder trembled. She gripped it for all she was worth. Now she could study the smears and scuff marks on his steel-toed work boots. Above her Nick breathed raggedly.

"You're an idiot," she told him conversationally, more to keep her brain engaged, thinking about the bigger picture than about what could happen if the beam slipped or he did.

"So—" he went up another step "—are you."

The boots went out of her line of sight. She had to look up if she wanted to see him at all. She did. The view was pretty spectacular—apart from the beam, which was downright scary.

She wanted to look away and was mesmerized at the same time. Nick was beginning to shift his weight, easing the beam forward off his shoulder and into place. As he did so, the ladder tilted. Edie clutched it with white-knuckled fingers, her breath caught in her throat.

And then he said, "Got it," and in the time-honored behavior of proficient ladder climbers everywhere, he skimmed back down before she could unlock her fingers from the uprights.

And there she stood, her hands locked to the ladder, her knees weak with relief, her nose pressed to the back of his neck, her arms bracketing him.

Exactly where she wanted to be.

She was so stunned she didn't move away. Just hung on. Clutched the ladder for dear life and breathed in the scent of sweat and dirt and something so elementally Nick.

For a moment Nick didn't move, either. He stayed absolutely motionless within her arms, as tense as she was boneless. She could see the tension in the quiver of the muscles of his back. Then his head dipped as he rested his forehead on one of the rungs and took a deep shuddering breath. The movement closed the millimeters of distance between her lips and the hard damp skin of his back.

She kissed it.

Tasted salt. Tasted Nick. Couldn't help herself.

It was a split second. That was all.

Yet at her touch he spun around. "God, Edie!"

Then he was kissing her back. Not a taste. He was determined to devour her. He wrapped her hard in his embrace and his mouth met hers with a fierce hunger. "Yes," he said, exultant. "Yes! I knew it. I told you." He pulled back to look at her, eyes glittering, triumphant.

And Edie grabbed for the shards of her sanity and shook her head. "No."

Hard fingers gripped her upper arms. "What do you mean, no? You kissed me!"

She wouldn't deny it. "Your neck," she said. "That's all."

"It's enough," he said. Then, "No, it's not. Not nearly. But you can't claim you don't want me."

"I never said that," Edie told him. "I did…want you," she admitted. She owed him that.

"Do," Nick corrected firmly, as if daring her to dispute it. "You do want me."

Edie pressed her lips together. "Yes," Edie admitted. "I do. But I told you—I want more than that." Her voice quieted. "And you don't." Their eyes met again and now she gave him a look that dared him to argue with her.

His teeth came together. A muscle in his jaw ticked. She dropped her gaze to watch the steady rise and fall of his hard, tanned chest. Then slowly she lifted her eyes once more. He met them squarely. He didn't say a word.

His silence said it all.

Somewhere in the treetops Edie could hear birds calling. A long way off the faint sound of a motorcycle broke the silence. By her knees Roy was panting.

She stepped back, drew in a breath and let it out slowly. "I have to go."

Nick's shoulders settled slightly. His fingers, which had been curled into fists, eased open and hung loosely at his sides. His dark eyes accused her.

She'd made the move. She'd changed her mind, they seemed to say.

She hadn't. She only wished she could.

CHAPTER SEVEN

THERE was gone—and then there was *gone*.

When Edie had said, "I have to go," Nick assumed she meant back to the house, back to the safety of her work schedule where she could pretend that the desire that had just flared up between them could be dialed back to a simmer she felt comfortable ignoring.

He didn't realize it meant she'd *left!*

But when he got back to the house that afternoon, still fuming, still horny, definitely determined to confront her, to tell her she could damned well stop saying one thing while her body wanted something else, she wasn't there.

Roy was there—in the house, waiting.

So was a note on the kitchen counter: *Out this evening. Lasagna in the refrigerator. I fed Roy.*

She hadn't even bothered to sign it.

An irritated breath hissed through Nick's teeth. He didn't eat the damned lasagna. It was Friday night. He wasn't going to spend it with a dog for company. He took a shower, then went into town in search of a good meal—and a little companionship. A woman. Someone to take his mind off Edie Daley.

If she wasn't going to share his bed, he was willing to bet he could find a woman who would.

He found a very good meal with no trouble at all. Santa Barbara had its share of fine dining. And afterward he met several young women at a sports bar just off State Street.

They were all too chattery and giggly or too blowsy and flirty. Their hair was too short or too blonde. They were too tall unless they were too short. Not one stirred his hormones in the slightest.

He drank a beer, talked a bit to the bartender and watched some baseball. Then, feeling more out of sorts than ever, he drove back to Mona's. Alone.

Roy was delighted. The dog wagged his tail madly, bumping his head against the back of Nick's thighs as he followed him into the sitting room. What it told Nick was that she hadn't come back yet. If she had, she would have reclaimed him.

It was past eleven. Hardly the witching hour, but where the hell was she?

He prowled the downstairs of the house, the dog at his heels. All evening he hadn't let himself wonder where she'd gone. It was her business. Not his. He didn't care.

Every time his thoughts had veered in her direction, he'd turned them away again or skipped right over them. Easy enough while he was watching the ball game. Not quite so simple when he was struck by the endless shortcomings of women who were not her. Even less so now that it was going on eleven-thirty and she wasn't here.

Did she expect him to babysit her dog all evening?

Nick jammed his hands into the pockets of his jeans and glowered out through the French doors at the sparkling turquoise of the pool set in the darkness of the garden. Then he jerked as his phone vibrated against his hand.

Surprised, he pulled it out of his pocket to stare at the number calling. It wasn't one he recognized.

He felt a quick skip beat of his heart as he flipped the phone open. "Savas. Where the hell are you?"

"Thailand. Where the hell are you?"

"Mona?"

It was, of course. No one else, not even Edie, had that sultry, sexy, immediately recognizable voice.

"Where are you?" she demanded again. "Are you in Santa Barbara? Working on the house? Where's Edie?" The questions came fast and furious.

Nick rubbed a hand against the back of his neck. "Yes, I'm in Santa Barbara," he said impatiently. "Yes, working on the house. And I don't know where Edie is."

"Why not?"

"I'm not her keeper," he snapped.

"No?" Mona said with just enough inflection in her voice to raise the hairs on the back of his neck.

"No," Nick said shortly.

"Whatever you say, dear." Mona brushed him off. "But you have seen her? She is there?"

"She was this afternoon," he said gruffly.

"Ah." One syllable. It was no wonder she was an actress. She could put layers of meaning into two letters.

Nick didn't reply. Wherever she was taking this conversation, he wasn't going willingly.

"Has something happened?" From her first fast and furious questions, Mona now sounded concerned.

Nick flexed his shoulders, kneaded the back of his neck, remembered that Edie's lips had touched him there and abruptly dropped his hand. "Happened? No, of course not."

Whatever happened—or hadn't—it was none of Mona's business.

"Well, she's not answering her phone," Mona said, clearly put out. "Edie *always* answers."

"That's ridiculous. It's almost midnight here," Nick reminded her. "She should have some time off. Maybe she's asleep."

"She'd hear her phone."

Or has a life, Nick wanted to press the issue, but didn't. Instead he said, "Maybe she didn't want to answer it."

Mona dismissed that idea with a mere *pffft* sound. "I need to talk to her. Tell her I need to talk to her."

"I'll tell her."

"Tell her to call me." And Mona rang off.

In the silence afterward, Nick stood glaring at the phone, not sure who he was most annoyed at—Edie or her mother.

Or himself—for not having taken up an invitation from one of the too giggly, too flirty, too blonde, too short or too tall women he'd met this evening.

Derek Saito was a nice guy. He was funny and charming and better looking than Edie remembered. He'd grown up, filled out and developed an easy, wry sense of humor since she and Ben had spent time with him back in their college days. He taught high school English, was unattached—"Heart whole"—he assured her, and he was obviously interested in her.

Equally obviously Derek was the steady nonmercurial sort of guy she should be interested in if she was seriously considering a relationship.

But she wasn't—interested, that is. Not in Derek.

It was as if the hormones that had been all wide-awake and raring to go when she'd been in Nick's arms this afternoon, had taken a sleeping potion as soon as Derek picked her up at her apartment.

Not just her hormones, either. Her brain.

They went out to dinner before the concert, and try as she might to follow Derek's conversational leads, her mind kept clicking back to that other man, the one who was going to walk out of her life sooner rather than later, the man who made it clear he wanted to bed her—but wanted nothing else.

She tried to keep focused, be alert, ask appropriate questions. But she knew she'd blown it when Derek, telling her about a summer high school theater production, asked if she'd read it.

She said, "Who wrote it?"

"Romeo and Juliet?" The pained smile on his face would stick in her mind forever. Or if it didn't, it should.

Her cheeks burned. "I'm sorry. I'm sorry. I don't know where my brain is. I—" she shook her head "—I haven't been sleeping well."

No lie there.

Derek's expression softened and he nodded understandingly. "I'm sure it's still difficult," he said, reaching across the table to give her hand a light pat. "I'm just glad you came out with me tonight."

"I am, too," Edie said fervently, though certainly not for the same reasons. "Which scenes are they doing?" she asked, and managed not to make any more grievous gaffes for the rest of the evening.

The concert was loud and raucous, but with enough beach and surf music as well as later rowdier stuff that meant pretty much everyone there had a good time.

Edie did, too. But she couldn't help wondering what sort of music Nick liked. They had never discussed music. And never would—because after today she was going to have to stay completely away from him until he finished the house.

Or maybe this time, she thought as Derek turned off the winding road and into the estate grounds, when she got home, he really would be gone.

The night was dark with a bit less than half a moon casting silver light amid deep shadows as they drove up the curving lane through the eucalyptus. Ahead, through the tree trunks, as they climbed the hill, Edie could see lights on in Mona's house. She reached for her purse on the floor of the car, and rehearsed her best, well-brought-up thank-you for the lovely evening speech as Derek took the last turn.

Nick's car was parked in front of the garage. The sight made her heart do a wholly undesirable cartwheel.

Deliberately she turned her attention on Derek. "It's been great."

He cut the engine and turned her way, smiling, too. "It has. I'm glad we did it."

She couldn't see his eyes, but she heard genuine friendliness in his voice, and perhaps a hint of regret. "So good to see you again. And the food was terrific."

Derek nodded. "Best place in town for fish tacos." His grin flashed in the moonlight. "Don't let anyone tell you I don't know how to give a girl a good time."

"It *was* a good time, Derek." She put her hand on the door handle. "Thank you."

He got out, too. She knew he would. Didn't know how to prevent it. Hoped he wouldn't be offended by the faintest of kisses good-night. Keeping a smile on her face, Edie headed toward the carriage house and stopping at the bottom of the steps, she turned. "Thank you again, Derek."

He smiled, a sort of wry, understanding smile. "It was my pleasure."

There was a moment when she thought she might not have to kiss him. But when he leaned in, she knew she couldn't turn her head away. It was the faintest brush. Nothing more. Her hormones didn't even notice.

"I'll ask my mother about talking to the class in the fall," she said. "But I don't know when I'll talk to her again. She doesn't seem to be answering her phone."

"Oh, she is now," a gruff, wholly unexpected voice said.

Edie jumped and spun around to see Nick come striding toward them out of the darkness. "She wants you to call her. Tonight."

She didn't know how he did it, but somehow he was standing between her and Derek, looming like some interfering father whose daughter had missed curfew.

"This is Nick Savas," she said to Derek. "He's working on restoring the old adobe ranch house. For my mother," she added pointedly, though she wasn't sure who she wanted to get the point—Derek or Nick.

"She wanted to know where you were," Nick went on as if she hadn't said a word. "Who you were out with." His tone made it clear he wasn't impressed with Derek.

"Thank you," Edie bit out. She didn't bother to introduce Derek. Nick was obviously in no mood to listen. "It was kind of you to stay up and relay the message—"

"Oh, I wasn't sleeping," Nick drawled. "I've been out. On the town. Just got home myself." He gave her a hard smile.

Edie felt the dart. He certainly hadn't wasted his time.

Derek, who had been watching their exchange as if they were on center court at Wimbledon, spoke up. "Well, don't let us keep you up," he said easily to Nick.

Edie looked at him in surprise and not a little admiration for his willingness to go nose to nose with Nick's impersonation of a pit bull guarding his bone.

Now Nick's teeth came together with a snap. His whole body seemed to almost vibrate with tension. And Edie thought that, interesting as it was, watching men trying to mark their territory, she really didn't much like being the "territory" in question.

And she didn't want Derek getting his butt kicked.

So she said to him, "I think I will just go call her now. How about if I call you in the morning and give you her answer?"

Derek seemed to hesitate a moment, but then nodded. "Appreciate it." His dark eyes held hers and he gave her a long, assessing look, as if he were reevaluating everything he'd thought earlier this evening.

As well he might.

Then he looked at Nick. "I'm a friend of Edie's—and her husband's," he added, establishing his right to be protective. The air seemed to hum between them. Then apparently Derek felt he'd made his point. He turned and walked back to his car.

Edie stood right where she was until Derek had got into his car, turned it round and driven off. Beside her, Nick stood like a sentry. She felt a serious urge to kick him.

"You could have waited," she said through her teeth.

Nick shrugged. "You could have said where you were going."

They didn't look at each other, both stood on the gravel in

the darkness watching Derek's car move down the hill around the bend until the taillights were out of sight.

Only then did Edie move away briskly toward Mona's house to get Roy. "I didn't imagine you'd care," she tossed over her shoulder.

"Your mother cared."

Her mother cared. He didn't. And that was the long and short of it, right there.

"I'll call her," Edie said, opening the door to Roy who shot out eagerly and danced around her. She ruffled his fur. "Come on then," she said.

With the dog by her side, she walked past Nick toward her apartment. All the way there, up the stairs, until the door shut behind her, she felt his eyes on her back.

"You rang," Edie said when her mother finally answered her phone. She said the words with considerably more acid than she usually used when talking to her mother. Ordinarily she simply smiled and let Mona's behavior, Mona's theories, Mona's view of the world sluice over her like water over a duck's back.

She'd learned long ago that she was her own person.

She just wished Mona would learn it, too.

"Are you all right?" her mother demanded now, surprising her.

There had been eleven messages from her mother when she'd got back to her apartment and turned on her phone. The first few had been long-winded directions of things Edie needed to do and who she needed to call if she hadn't done so already (which she had).

After the fifth the messages began to get shorter and edgier, until the last one said, "My God, Edie! Answer your phone or I'll think you're dead!"

"I'm fine," Edie said. "I had a date."

"Nick said he didn't know where you were." Mona's annoyance came through loud and clear.

"I wasn't out with Nick," Edie said through her teeth. "And I don't need you throwing men at me!"

There was a moment's silence and then Mona said, "What?"

"You heard me," Edie said, fed up with guilelessness that was anything but. Her mother might be an award winning actress, but she couldn't fool Edie. "I said I don't need you throwing men at me! I know you think I should date again. I know you think I need to get on with my life. But understand one thing, it's my life! I'll find my own man when I want one!"

This time the silence lasted longer. Then Mona said almost meekly, "I'm sure you will."

Edie ground her teeth. "I mean it. I thought I'd made it clear after the night of the wedding in Mont Chamion. Didn't you hear anything I said?"

"You said," Mona parroted carefully, "I don't want you finding men for me. I especially don't want you setting me up with Kyle Robbins. Do not ever do that again."

It was a scarily accurate impersonation of the short version of what Edie had said to her mother that night.

"And?" Edie pressed when Mona didn't say anything else.

"Don't tell me you went out with Kyle Robbins?"

"No, damn it! I didn't go out with Kyle. Did you send him, too?"

"Too?"

"Besides Nick," Edie spat, furious that Mona wouldn't just admit to setting her up. Again.

"Say what?"

"Why else would he be here?" Edie demanded.

"Well, when he called, he said he was interested in looking at the house I'd told him about," Mona replied.

Edie opened her mouth. No sound came out. *He'd* called Mona? He'd said...*what?*

"*Nick* called? You?"

"Nick called me," Mona affirmed.

"You...didn't call him?"

"Edie."

"I'm just…trying to understand." Edie thought she must have been standing too long. Her knees felt wobbly. She sat down and tried to think.

"I should think it would be obvious," Mona said dryly.

Was it?

Edie shook her head. "No," she said, the single word soft and uncertain.

"Oh, for goodness' sake," Mona said, exasperated. "Why do you think he wanted to renovate my tumbling down adobe ranch house? To pad his résumé? To impress another king? I suppose you imagine an inconsequential ranch is going to do that? I don't think so!"

"But then—"

"He came for you." Mona put it in words of one syllable.

"But—" Once more Edie stopped, dazed, shaking her head. She'd jumped to that conclusion herself when he'd appeared on the doorstep. Her heart had leaped. Her hopes had danced. And then she'd asked, "What are you doing here?"

And Nick had replied…?

What *had* Nick replied?

She racked her brain. He'd said nothing direct at all. No straight out statement that he'd come for her. But no denial, either. He'd said, *I've been talking to your mother.*

Edie went perfectly still, tried to think it through. Didn't breathe. Didn't dare hope.

And yet…

"Edie?"

She was still thinking. Her mind whirled. It didn't make sense. Why would he have suggested he renovate the adobe unless…?

"Are you sure he called you?" she asked her mother.

"What is going on there?" Mona demanded. "Should I have said no? You went off with him the night I 'threw' Kyle at you," she reminded Edie forcefully. "I thought you liked him."

"I barely knew him," Edie said. "Then," she added hastily, lest her mother get even worse ideas than she was already apparently entertaining. "And yes, I—I like him."

"So," Mona said archly, "I'm forgiven?"

Edie supposed she was lucky her mother wasn't asking for an apology from her! "Yes," she said. "As long as you don't do it again."

"I'm hoping I won't have to." Mona's meaning was crystal clear.

"It's...not as simple as you might think," Edie said.

"I know you loved Ben—"

"This isn't about Ben," Edie said.

"Because loving Ben is no excuse to turn your back on life," Mona went on as if Edie hadn't spoken. "I loved your father with all my heart." She stopped abruptly, and Edie was surprised to hear a break in her mother's voice that had nothing to do with Mona's legendary acting ability. "I loved him," she said again, more quietly, but no less fervently.

"I know that, Mom," Edie said. "I've always known it."

But she was grateful for the words all the same. Mona so rarely stopped to look back that it was good to hear that reaffirmation. "But," she said again, "this isn't about Ben. Or Dad."

"Then what's it about?" Except in her layered acting performances, Mona wasn't one for subtlety.

"It's about Nick."

"What about Nick?"

Indeed, what about Nick? "That's what I'm trying to figure out. I'll call you back in the morning. My morning or your morning or something," Edie qualified. "I'm tired now. I've got to sleep. And I've got to think."

"Try not to do both at the same time," Mona said dryly.

But she didn't make any more comments—and she let the myriad work questions slide. All she said was, "If you need to talk, Edie..."

"Thanks," Edie said absently, already thinking. It wasn't

Mona she needed to talk to. Still. "Thanks, Mom," she said now because for once the term seemed right.

They called it a paradigm shift.

When phenomena could not be explained by the laws of the world as one knew it, one had to rethink.

That night Edie rethought.

She lay in bed and stared at the ceiling and looked at the events of the past week through a lens created by a new piece of information: Nick was the one who had called her mother, not the other way around.

Nick was the one who had proposed coming to see the house, to evaluate it, to see if it was worth renovating it.

Why?

Mona admitted having told him it existed. Edie knew that already. When they came back, she had handed Edie a piece of paper Nick had given here with the names of a couple of possible architects she might want to call to see if they'd be interested in the project.

But instead he came himself.

Why?

Because he desperately wanted to renovate an old adobe ranch house?

Hardly. Mona was right in scorning that notion. Owners of significant old buildings worldwide regularly attempted to hire Nick Savas. When she'd come home from Mont Chamion, despite her better judgment, which told her to forget him, Edie had looked him up on the internet instead. Nick Savas was a recognized, sought-after authority in architectural reconstruction and renovation. He could—and did—have his pick of projects.

So why had he picked this one?

If Mona had asked him, he might have considered it. There was, Edie knew, no discounting the pull of her mother's star power. But since Mona hadn't asked—and Edie trusted that she hadn't—it made no sense.

Unless Nick had another reason for coming.

Her.

The thought felt odd—daring—and came with the expectation of being slapped down for even venturing to voice it. After all, that was the unspoken hope she'd felt when he showed up at the door.

And he'd shot it down with very nearly his first words.

Why?

Because she'd shown that hope. She'd indicated that she cared and could care even more, and Nick hadn't wanted that. He wanted a physical relationship, and nothing else.

But when she said no to that, he could have left. He could have said the adobe wasn't worth saving. He could have said he didn't have time. But he didn't say that.

He stayed. Which meant…

Edie felt a renewed shiver of hope as she pushed that idea to its conclusion: whether he wanted to or not, Nick Savas cared—about her.

He hadn't stayed for the joy of working on a project he could easily have passed over. He hadn't stayed for the red-hot sex they were having—because they weren't having any.

He'd stayed for her.

It was about that point—at 3:12 in the morning, according to the bedside clock—that Edie realized she was grinning madly at the ceiling. She stopped grinning. Now was not the time to grin.

Now was the time to think some more, to figure out what to do next—because if Nick really cared, it changed everything.

Nick's stomach was not happy.

Neither was Nick, but that was beside the point.

What *was* the point was that he was starving. He'd grabbed a bagel and some coffee at seven after a not particularly restful night spent wondering what the hell was going on between Edie and the man who'd brought her home, and it was now going on two in the afternoon, and he'd left his lunch at Mona's.

He wasn't going back after it, either. If he did, Edie would doubtless think he'd done it on purpose so he could come back to check up on her. Or maybe she wasn't even there. It was Saturday, after all. She probably took weekends off.

She'd certainly taken Friday night off!

Then he reminded himself for the hundredth time that what she did was her own business, damn it. Just like he'd told her mother. But he didn't like Mr. Proprietary's "I'm a friend of hers—and her husband's." As if that meant he had rights Nick didn't have.

Nick wished he were doing something more physical and demanding than setting tiles on the roof. Tearing out a wall sounded like a far more satisfying occupation.

He pulled a bandanna from his pocket and wiped the sweat off his face, and was just putting another tile in place when a voice called out, "Hungry?"

His head whipped around. For a moment he thought he was hearing things. His stomach growled as if in reply. And then he heard footsteps as well and looking around, he saw Edie and Roy coming down the hill through the eucalyptus.

She was wearing canvas knee-length shorts and a bright green T-shirt, not the sort of casual, but professional, attire she wore during the workweek, so she must in fact have the day off. Her hair was pulled back and banded at the nape of her neck. She wore a floppy red straw sunhat on her head, and she was carrying a basket over her arm. When she reached the front yard she squinted up at him on the roof. "You forgot your lunch."

"Yeah."

"So I brought it." She shrugged, smiling. "And mine, too."

Hers? Nick's brows lifted, then his eyes narrowed.

Edie didn't move, just kept smiling, kept looking up at him. He didn't move, either. There was something wrong with the picture. His brain was scrambling to figure out what it was. Last night she'd been spitting nails at him. And today she was…

"Or maybe you're not hungry," she said when he stayed where he was. "Oh, well. You don't mind if I eat here, do you?"

And with that, she carried the basket up the plank he'd laid over the broken steps and disappeared into the house.

If he'd been a weather vane on this roof, Nick figured he'd have been blown around about 180 degrees. He rubbed his head. It was hot and the sun was beating down. Maybe he had sunstroke. He gave his head a little shake, then picked up a tile again.

His stomach growled.

"Oh, hell," he muttered. "All right."

It was all right, too. He expected either an apology for snarling and spitting at him last night or more snarling and spitting today. But he didn't get either. He got little Miss Mary Sunshine.

Cheerful, bright, tart, funny—not to mention as appealing as ever, Edie was once again the woman he'd spent that unforgettable night with in Mont Chamion.

She'd brought his sandwiches and his apple. But she'd added a thermos of iced tea, a couple of bottles of cold beer and some potato salad. "I wasn't sure what you brought to drink at lunch," she said. "So I brought both. And I was feeling domestic this morning, so I made some salad."

She'd cleared off the kitchen table, where he'd laid hammers and rasps and a crowbar, and had wiped it down with a damp cloth. She set it with paper plates and forks for the salad, and sat down as he came in, then gestured at the place opposite for him to take a seat.

Somewhere amid wary, perplexed, bemused and intrigued, Nick sat.

She told him she had talked to her mother. That was as close as she came to acknowledging their encounter last night.

"She's very enthusiastic about the renovation," she told him brightly, and her own eyes were shining. "But since you talked to her, you obviously know that."

He and Mona hadn't talked about the adobe at all, in fact. The only reason Mona had called had been to demand to know where Edie was. But that would have meant talking about how he'd come to be here in the first place, and Nick didn't want to get into that again. So he simply nodded and washed a bite of his sandwich down with a long swallow of beer. He didn't bring beer to work, but it was Saturday—and if Edie was going to bring it, well, he wouldn't say no.

"Are you working all day?" she asked.

"You got a better idea?" He grinned, expecting her to get flustered.

But she said, "I was thinking of going to the beach."

"With lover boy?" Nick bit out before he could stop himself.

Edie blinked, looking momentarily confused, then said, "You mean Derek?" She shook her head. "No. I was going by myself. Unless you want to come." She made the invitation offhandedly, then got up and fetched herself a glass of water from the sink.

Nick hesitated. Then he nodded. "I wouldn't mind. Got a bit to finish up here first. An hour?"

"Perfect." Edie's smile flashed again as she got up and started gathering up the paper plates and silverware to carry out in the basket.

Nick finished his apple, drained his bottle of beer, then headed outside to go up the ladder again. But before he got to the door, he turned back. "Thanks for lunch." He paused, then had to ask, "What's changed?"

Edie finished putting the bowl of salad and the other things back into the basket before she looked up. "Changed?" Her tone was just a little too casual.

So he pressed. "You were avoiding me. Now you're not."

She smiled faintly. Her gaze warmed and under the heat of it, so did he. "No," she allowed slowly, "I'm not."

"Because," he prompted when she didn't elaborate.

Edie ran her tongue over her lips, then shrugged and met his gaze head-on. "Because I only have one life," she said quietly.

CHAPTER EIGHT

THEY went to Leadbetter's Beach where Edie used to go to when she was in high school.

It was a city beach not far from the marina, a picture post-card sort of place with light surf, white sand and blue skies in one direction, and the Spanish architecture and red tile roofs of the city and hills of Santa Barbara in the other. She chose it because it was a place where she had good memories, but wasn't where she habitually went with Ben.

Nick enjoyed it, as she'd hoped he would. They swam, they bodysurfed, they walked on the beach. Edie hadn't known if he was a "beach person" or not. There was so much she still had to learn about him. She was eager to know more.

And she was glad that she had found the courage to do it. Glad that what Mona told her gave her a promise to build on. She could work with that.

Thanks to Ben she knew how. He had done the same for her.

After her painful unrequited love affair with Kyle, Edie had shied away from men, afraid to trust, scared of putting her heart on the line.

She'd resisted Ben. "I don't want to go out," she told him more than once. "I don't want to get involved."

Ben had just looked at her and smiled. Then he'd said, "Let's go ride some waves," or "Let's go fly a kite."

Ben had been full of suggestions. But he only suggested. He

never demanded. And in the face of such good-natured perseverance, Edie hadn't been able to resist.

They had done simple things together. They'd gone to the beach, went for bike rides, raked leaves, cooked meals.

They were friends first.

Perhaps that was why it had worked—*because* they had been friends since grade school. They'd been friends long before they were anything else. And that easy friendship had given Edie a chance to be with Ben in circumstances that, at first, didn't feel like dates.

"No expectations," he had promised her solemnly. But then he'd grinned. "Which doesn't mean I'm not hoping."

Edie understood. And the truth was, she felt something, too, something initially less heated and consuming than the sizzle she'd felt with Kyle, but still real. More real, if possible, because what she and Ben nourished together didn't flare brightly, then scorch and die.

The more time they were together, the stronger it grew.

It was different with Nick, of course. He wasn't Ben. They hadn't known each other forever. They hadn't been friends.

Before everything else, they had been lovers.

And from that very moment there had been something between them—a spark, a hum, a hint, a promise.

She'd tried to ignore that promise, but it hadn't gone away. And now she was no longer determined to resist it. On the contrary, she was making the choice Nick had told her was hers to make.

Not whether or not to fall in love with him—that had already happened. But whether to run from it or to try to create a relationship from it—that was her choice. And she chose to stop running, to turn and hold out her arms.

And Nick?

Nick was where she'd been before Ben had brought her back to life. He was locked in the past with the pain of his fiancée's death. He had turned his back on hope, on dreams, on possibilities.

And yet, he felt something for her. She was sure of it. If he didn't, he wouldn't have come.

It was a very slim hope on which to begin to build a future.

She should be afraid, Edie told herself. Risking your heart wasn't for sissies. But she knew from loving Ben it was worth the cost.

And if Nick didn't know that, well, she'd just have to teach him.

Nick didn't know why Edie had changed her mind.

But he was damned glad she had. Since she'd stopped going out of doors when he came in them, stopped being distantly polite when they talked and started coming around to see how things were going on the adobe restoration and actually stayed to talk about what she remembered about growing up there, the days got a whole lot brighter.

And the nights? Well, the nights were everything he'd imagined.

Nick hadn't known what to expect about the nights—or rather what Edie intended to do about them. It didn't take him long to find out.

That very evening after dinner she put the last of the dishes in the dishwasher, then said, "I was thinking I might take a swim."

"Swim?" He'd been thinking about how to convince her to stay around, talk a bit longer, hoping her change of heart wouldn't have her heading off right after dinner. And now she was suggesting a swim?

She nodded and smiled an even more dazzling smile than the one she'd given him when she'd hooked her arm through his that night in Mont Chamion. "Join me?"

She didn't have to ask him twice.

The night was clear and still warm though the sun still hung like a great orange ball above the city's rooftops and the sea.

Edie had gone back to her place to change, but as Nick headed toward the pool, she ran past him down the sloping lawn. "Can't catch me," she sang.

Grinning, Nick watched her run. He had seen the look on her face well enough to recognize the promise. He didn't hurry. There would be time.

When he got there she was already churning through the water, doing laps. He settled himself on the side of the pool and dangled his feet over the edge as he watched her lithe form cutting through the cool turquoise water.

Several laps done, she veered off course and swam over to look up at him. "That's not swimming," she said.

"I'm watching." He smiled. "And conserving my energy."

She tossed her hair back out of her face, a smile touching her lips. "Think you're going to need it?"

"Hoping."

Their eyes met. Gazes locked for a brief moment.

"Me, too," Edie said quietly, and Nick felt his body go hard in an instant. Then quick as a flash Edie's body bent. She ducked her head and dived beneath the water. A hand caught his ankle, gave a hard tug and pulled him in!

By the time he sputtered to the surface, she was half a width of the pool away.

Grinning, Nick swam after her. Again he didn't hurry. The anticipation was part of the game.

It was a game—and more than that, too. She was grinning as he caught her, laughing as he pulled her back against him, then turned her in his arms and set his mouth on hers. He meant to tease, to taste, to tempt. To play her game and raise the stakes a bit.

But it had been so long since he had held her—really held her. His hands moved up her back, sliding over the wet silk of her skin to press her close. His tongue traced her lips, opened them, delved in. One kiss wasn't enough. Nor two, nor three. Kisses would never be enough. He groaned.

"You're supposed to swim," she said against his lips.

He shook his head. "Can't. I'm drowning." In desire. In sensation. In need. In *her*. "Edie." His hands moved down now to splay across her bottom and press her closer, let her feel how urgently he wanted her.

Her legs twined around his, bringing him still closer, pressing them together. Her hands clutched his shoulders as her heels bumped the backs of his knees. His thumbs hooked the back of her bikini and began to draw it down, his fingers smoothing over the curve of her buttocks as he did so. Edie pulled back, shifted a little, letting go of him with first one leg and then the other, so he could slide the garment down until she could kick it away.

Then his hands moved back up her legs, teased her inner thighs, brushed the soft folds at their apex, then stroked her there.

It was Edie's turn to groan, to wrap her legs around him and press her mouth to his, to devour him as hungrily as he was kissing her. But still it wasn't enough. She squirmed against his touch. She pressed harder. His fingers slipped inside her and he felt her clench around them.

"Nick!"

"Mmm." He wanted her badly. But to take her now would be a matter of moments. He had waited too long, knew that he would shatter at the merest touch. Now...now he wanted to give to her, to prove to her that she had made the right choice.

So when her hands had slid down his arms to reach his waist, intent on slipping beneath his trunks to free him, he stopped her.

"But—" Edie protested.

"There will be time. This is for you." Then the only things that moved were his fingers, giving her pleasure, making her dig her heels into the backs of his thighs, making her arch her back and let her head fall back. He felt her body tense, clench and shudder against him. Then her head came forward, her forehead dropping on his shoulder as she collapsed against him. Then the only thing moving was the lap of cool water against fevered bodies—and the pounding of their hearts.

Edie moved first, shifted slowly in his arms, would have pulled away, but he was loathe to let her go. He liked the warmth of her, the weight of her in his embrace. So he held on, but lightly, giving her space. She didn't take much, just enough to stroke a hand down his chest. "That was—" she shook her head "—amazing."

"Better than swimming?"

She smiled, kissed his jaw. "Oh, yes." Her hand stole lower, brushed across the front of his swim trunks. "And now?"

"Not here," Nick said, lifting her and settling her on the side of the pool, then hauling himself out as well. "I think we could use a bed for the second round."

Edie's eyes widened, her mouth laughed. "We're having rounds? How many?"

He kissed her. "As many as we can get."

Edie didn't regret changing her mind. If she regretted anything, it was that she hadn't changed it sooner. If she'd been braver, they could have had spent more days together at the adobe, more nights sharing a bed.

But they were together now. They spent a lot of every day together. The beauty of her job was that she could do it from almost anywhere. So while Nick worked on the adobe, most afternoons now Edie took her cell phone and her laptop, and she and Roy went over the hill to bring Nick lunch and spend the afternoon with him.

They ate together, sitting on the front porch if it was cool, or inside with fans on if it was a bit too warm. And she asked questions about what he was doing and he asked questions about what she remembered.

The more they talked, the more she was able to explain the hold the house had on her. It was, as she told him, "where it all began." It was a reminder of the core values of love and commitment and allegiance to family that her parents had given her. They were values she wanted to share with her own children, values she wanted to share with Nick.

She didn't say so outright. She simply explained the best she could.

"It's a touchstone," Nick said.

She nodded. "Exactly. The best of times," she reflected, but then remembered the day the sheriff's car had driven up and the man had got out to talk to her mother. Her smile faded. "And the worst of times," she whispered.

But then Nick took her hands in his and leaned over to kiss her. "We'll make it right," he vowed against her lips.

He made her happy. Whatever else he did, Nick Savas did that.

He seemed to delight in making her smile. He even went so far as to figure out what mattered to her without her even telling him. She mentioned once how she'd love to play on the high, wide back porch under the kitchen windows.

"It was my place," she told him. "Ronan preferred trees. But I loved it there. I played house there and school there, with my friend Katie. It was special because I could be on my own. My mom only had to look out the window."

Thinking about it now, it seemed strange that international movie star Mona Tremayne had once been just like all the other moms who kept an eye on her children. But she had—at the same time she'd known to give her daughter space.

"I'd like to do that for my children," she'd reflected.

The next day when she came back with lunch, he said, "Why don't we eat out on the back porch?"

"It's filthy," she protested, because it certainly had been the day before.

But when she came through the house into the kitchen, the back door stood open onto a porch of brand-new wood. Edie let out a little scream. She dumped the basket on the table and hurried outside, looking all around.

"Oh! Oh, yes!" Her eyes were shining as she spun around. "Yes, exactly! And the stairs—" She crossed the porch and peered down the back steps. There had been six of them, she'd told Nick yesterday. They'd played school on them—each stair being assigned a different grade. Now she counted them, then turned back to him, beaming. "Six! It's perfect!" She knelt down and ran her hands over the sanded wood. "Better than," she told him, "because the old wood was rough and we were always getting splinters."

"No splinters in this," Nick assured her.

"Thank you." She flung her arms around him and kissed him hard. He returned the kiss with equal fervency—and she suspected that things would have got scandalous then and there, but he pulled back, grimacing and said, "I've got a couple of plasterers coming after lunch."

"Bad planning," Edie told him, laughing.

"I'll make it up to you tonight."

"Is that a threat or a promise?"

"What do you think?"

Edie thought life was wonderful—and getting better by the minute. "I'll be looking forward to it," she told him, getting out a cloth to spread on the new wood so they could picnic there. Afterward she left him to his plasterers and took Roy back home for the afternoon. But before she left she turned to him and took his hands in hers, then looked up into his eyes.

"Thank you for the porch, Nick. I love it."

He nodded. "I'm glad."

"My children thank you, too."

He blinked. But he didn't say anything else because she went up on her toes and kissed him.

Her children?

He'd done it for her—for the memories she had told him

about—and now all he could envision were her children. Little dark-haired girls and grinning boys with freckled noses.

It made him hot—and cold—at the very same time. He'd never thought about Edie in the future before. It had always been now—and the two of them—together.

But suddenly he could see her surrounded by children.

Whose?

He shook the question off as soon as it occurred to him. It didn't matter, he told himself. It wasn't his problem. They weren't his children.

But the notion stuck with him all afternoon. The plasterers showed up and they discussed how to best deal with the interior walls. He'd intended to have them working in the bedrooms. Now, walking into Edie's old room, he imagined it not as hers but as the room her daughters might use. And Ronan's bedroom somehow seemed to be populated by little boys who would be Edie's sons.

He didn't hear everything the plasterers said. He wasn't sure he communicated at all what he wanted them to do. They said, "Sure. Fine," and they could start on Monday. He said uh-huh or something like that.

He was glad when they left. He left right after they did, heading back to Mona's earlier than usual.

Edie was on the phone. She looked up surprised when he came in. She waggled her fingers at him and smiled, then kept listening, occasionally murmuring something that sounded comforting.

He was grimy and sweaty, and on the way back to the house he'd been planning for Edie to take a shower with him and wash his back. But now she was obviously deep in a conversation, so he went up the stairs by himself, took a quick shower, put on clean clothes and went back down.

She was still listening. And listening. She was moving around the kitchen as she did so, putting together something for dinner. But her attention was obviously on the person she was talking to.

"I know," she was saying. "Yes, I remember."

Nick ambled out to the den to turn on the television and catch up on the baseball scores. It was another half an hour before Edie joined him.

"Grace," she said by way of explanation.

"From Thailand?"

She nodded. "Her boyfriend dumped her."

"She had a boyfriend in Thailand."

"No. Here. He read something in some gossip blog online about her and Matt Holden. He's an actor," she explained, in case he didn't know. He'd heard the name, but that was about it. "About twenty. A heartthrob-to-be. David took exception."

Why this was Edie's problem, Nick had no idea. But obviously she'd spent a long time talking to and listening to her sister. And he could tell from her expression and the few remarks she made that it was important, that Grace mattered. All her siblings mattered.

Edie wasn't just her mother's and Rhiannon's business manager. She was the glue that held the family together, the one that everyone turned to when things went awry.

Rhiannon, he realized, had things go awry on a regular basis. A day rarely went by that he didn't overhear Edie soothing and settling her sister, making arrangements and then rearranging them with what seemed like endless patience and good cheer when Rhiannon couldn't manage to make things work.

Mona made fewer demands. Her requests were generally in line with the work Edie was hired for. But the younger children—Grace and the twins, Ruud and Dirk—all turned to Edie, not their mother, for support. They might have been half a world away in Thailand, but they called Edie almost every day. She might as well have been their mother. She would make a wonderful mother.

And there he was, facing the Edie of the future again.

"Do you expect to live in the adobe?" he demanded.

She was going back into the kitchen to put the pan of lasagna she'd been making into the oven. But now she stopped and looked at him surprised. But then she tilted her head and seemed to give it serious thought.

"I hadn't thought about it recently," she said. "Until today. But since there's such a nice new back porch..." She nodded. "Yes, I think so. Not all the time, of course. I would hope to have a place *not* at my mother's. But it would be a good place to bring the family, don't you think?"

Fortunately she didn't wait for a reply, which was just as well, as he didn't have an answer.

"That way the kids could be near Mona and not be underfoot. Good for everyone concerned," she added with a smile. "Mona loves kids, but the day to day isn't really her style."

But it was Edie's style. And now that Nick could see it, he couldn't seem to forget it, especially because, besides Grace's ongoing soap opera, later in the week Edie spent an evening talking to Dirk who was trying to set up a connection so he could listen to baseball games from Bangkok. Between the two of them, they accomplished the task—fortunately right before Nick carried her off to bed.

"You're very eager," she commented as he drew her with him up the stairs.

"I am." He was kissing her as they went, then tugging her scoop-necked T-shirt over her head.

"Why is that?" she asked, though she seemed to be equally eager, fumbling to undo the button at the waistband of his shorts.

"Can't get enough of you," he murmured, bearing her back onto the bed.

He didn't know why it was true. He only knew it was. The more time he spent with Edie—in bed and out—the more he wanted to be with her. He certainly hadn't tired of her. If he was going to get his fill of Edie Daley, he was going to need every available minute between now and when the restoration was done.

Getting his fill wasn't easy to imagine. He kept devising

more and more ways to spend time in her company. They spent lunches together, afternoons at the adobe, dinners every evening and nights in her bed or his. Far more time than he had ever spent with anyone.

But far from sating his desire to be with her, he was annoyed one afternoon at the end of the third week they'd shared, when she packed up the lunch basket and said she'd see him at dinner.

"Dinner?" he frowned. "Where are you going?"

He was surprised how much it mattered. But he'd grown used to having her there. Until Edie he'd never invited anyone to be there while he was working. Not even Amy when he'd been building the house he'd designed for her.

Nick willingly listened to other peoples' input. He valued their ideas, but he didn't like interference, and he'd always worked alone. So he was probably more surprised than Edie the first afternoon he'd suggested she stay. And he was equally surprised now to discover that he cared when she wasn't going to be here today.

"I promised Ruud that I'd get the skateboard wheels he wants and put them in the mail this afternoon."

Of course it would be on account of one of her siblings. He should have known. Still he raised his brows. "You know skateboards?" He understood now that there was quite a bit more to Edie Daley than he'd first imagined, but—skateboards?

She smiled. "I have explicit instructions." And she pulled a paper out of the pocket of her shorts and waved it at him.

Nick took the paper and scanned it over. "How will you choose? He's got four different options."

"I'm supposed to pick the best." She sighed. "He's got them ranked. Or, he said I could ask someone who knew something." She looked at him hopefully. "What do you know about skateboards?"

Nick grinned. "I rode my share in olden times."

"Really?" She was delighted. "Come with me, then. I could use an expert."

He hadn't ridden a skateboard since he was in his teens. He was a Neanderthal in the skateboard world.

But if it meant spending the day with Edie…

"All right." Something else he rarely did, take time off during the workweek. When a man worked for himself, he had to be a tough taskmaster.

So he made it a work trip, stopping at the building supply place and picking up some materials as well. But after they'd checked several skate shops and picked his choice of the perfect wheels, then mailed them, Edie suggested they go for a walk along the beach before going back to the house.

"It's beautiful down here. And it's too late to go back to the adobe and work. It's nearly five. We can take a walk, then stop somewhere for an early supper." She turned to him, eyes shining, and said, "We could go to the Biltmore."

The Biltmore was an old Santa Barbara landmark right on the beach just a ways down the coast from downtown. Built in the 1920s at the height of Santa Barbara's determined celebration of its Spanish colonial heritage, the Biltmore embodied what idealists believed neo-Colonial buildings should look like. With its thick adobe style walls, red-tile roof, wrought-iron gates and Moorish archways, the place looked more like a romantic movie set than a hotel.

"Think of it as inspiration," Edie said, grinning.

For once Nick couldn't think of a reason to argue. He shrugged and laced his fingers through hers. "Why not?"

Tempting fate—that's what it was—asking Nick to go to the Biltmore.

But the words were out of her mouth before Edie could stop them. Truth was, she didn't want to stop them. She wanted to go to the Biltmore with him, have a meal there with him, wanted to share the romantic ambiance, the special setting and—this was the part that tempted fate—add to the family history in the process.

The Biltmore was where she had come with Ben to celebrate their engagement. It was, thirty odd years ago, where her parents had had dinner the night that Joe had asked Mona to marry him. It was where, thirty years before that, Joe's own mother and father had met when she was working in the kitchen and he was the chauffeur of a wealthy Bostonian who had come west to spend the winter in milder climes.

Memorable days at the Biltmore were something of a family tradition.

Not that Edie told Nick that.

She certainly didn't intend to ask him to marry her there—and she would be shocked if he asked her. Not tonight. Not yet. But soon.

Yes, she dared to hope it would be soon.

What they'd shared these past weeks had not weakened, had not diminished. It had only grown. The time they spent together, the tales she told him of her childhood and the stories of his youth that Nick shared, showed her how much common ground they had. They had as well a love of history, an appreciation of family, friends and big black dogs, of restoring houses and swimming races, of walks on the beach and picnics between mornings and afternoons working, and nights in each other's arms.

They'd both loved—and they'd both lost. She didn't expect to replace Amy in his heart any more than she knew he could ever replace Ben. There was room for both. In her perhaps foolish, but still admirable willingness to risk again and again, Mona had shown her that. Ben had taught her to trust, to dare to love.

She *loved* Nick.

Back in Mont Chamion, she'd told herself she wouldn't. When he'd first come to Santa Barbara and had promised nothing but the moment, she'd resisted. Or tried to.

But she couldn't resist forever. Didn't want to.

She loved him.

And, yes, perhaps it was tempting fate to suggest the Biltmore, to know in her heart what that meant, but she couldn't help it.

Edie believed. Edie hoped.

They parked the car across the street from the hotel, next to the sidewalk that ran along the beach. Because it was still too early for dinner, they took off their shoes and climbed over the low wall to walk on the beach. It was when she was jumping off the wall that he caught her and, afterward, hung on, that kept her hand in his.

Edie smiled and rubbed her thumb along the side of his hand and tipped her face to let the afternoon sun warm her even as Nick warmed her heart. They walked all the way to the marina and back, holding hands, hips brushing. They talked as they walked, shared stories, laughter. And then there were times they walked in silence. Both were comfortable, both felt right.

And when they got back to the Biltmore, they wiped their feet and put their shoes back on, and Edie combed her hair. She had no doubt that her grandparents would have been scandalized at the lack of dress code at the Biltmore these days. Some things had indeed changed.

But others—like two people staring into each other's eyes over a candlelight dinner—had not.

The meal was lovely—fresh caught seafood, pasta cooked to order, fresh salad greens. The wine was superb. Nick chose it, raised his glass and clinked it against hers, his gaze smoldering as he said, "To you, Ms. Daley." His voice was ragged.

Edie raised her own glass, looking deep into his eyes. "To you, Mr. Savas." In her heart she said, *To us.*

They skipped dessert. All the tortes and flans and tarts and cheesecakes looked delicious. The zabaglione, Edie knew from experience, was to die for. But she didn't even hesitate tonight.

Something better waited for them at home.

They barely spoke as Nick drove them back. He held her hand even as he drove. The only time he let go was when they reached the house and they got out of opposite sides of the car. But Nick caught her hand in his before they climbed the stairs.

They had made love in his bed in her old room in Mona's

house. They had made love by the pool. Once they had even made love at the adobe on the old madras cotton bedspread Edie had brought to lay out their picnics on.

But mostly they came here—to her bed. And while Edie would have loved Nick anywhere, she liked making love with him here best.

Her carriage house flat was small and not at all lavish. But it was her home and, as much as anywhere on earth, it held pieces of her heart. Here was the photo of her dad with his arms around her and Ronan, taken on Christmas morning, just a month before he died. Here was the photo of Mona with all her children around her—a motley crew, but deeply beloved. Here were the memories she had of Ben—a carving he'd done for her when they'd lived in Fiji, a tiny outrigger he'd made when he'd been researching on one of the small islands and she'd spent three whole weeks without him, a box containing all the postcards she'd sent her mother while she and Ben were abroad. Mona had given them to her just last year.

"Because you can handle remembering now," her mother had said. "You can look back with love. And you can move on."

At the time Edie hadn't been sure. But though Mona's gift might have been a bit premature, she was right. Edie was ready now. And she was glad Nick was willing to make love to her here.

Roy went shooting out the door the minute they came in. But in a few minutes, he was back looking for dinner. Gerald, the cat, meowed plaintively and wove his way between their feet, indignant that he hadn't had his evening meal.

"I know you're hungry," Edie said to him. She reached for his bowl and a can of cat food.

Nick stood behind her, kissing her neck, making her shiver with longing. His hands played lightly over her breasts. "In case you haven't noticed," he murmured, "I'm hungry, too."

"Gerald would say you had a wonderful meal," Edie told him,

opening the can and scooping food into the dish. "Fresh sword-fish. Yum."

"To a neutered feline, the food of gods, no doubt." Nick nibbled along the her partially exposed shoulder. "I've got better things to feast on."

She put the dish of food down for the cat, and felt herself scooped into Nick's arms and carried through to the bedroom.

Nick dropped her lightly onto the bed, then fell down beside her, stroked her clothes off and in a matter of moments shed his own. Then, at her urging, he settled his hard muscled body over hers. And Edie opened to him, wrapped her arms around his neck and let him feast his fill.

They loved with fierce intensity, their bodies hot and slick with sweat as they drove each other to frenzied completion. But after their coupling, neither of them slept. They held each other close. They slept and woke and loved again, then slept some more.

It was close to dawn when she stroked his whisker roughened jaw. He threaded his fingers through her hair. She kissed her way along his collarbone, then down the center of his chest, to nuzzle his navel, then moved lower.

Nick sucked in a sharp breath. "You're going to kill me," he said raggedly.

"I'm hungry, too." Edie lifted her head to look at him through the curtain of her hair. Then she went back to kissing and nibbling, touching him with her tongue, making him groan, wringing him out, until he pulled her up and settled her over him and drew her down to take him in.

His breath hissed between his teeth as she rode him.

They shattered together, and Edie collapsed against him, heard his heart thundering against her ear. His arms held her close, circled her back, his lips pressed against her hair.

"Dear God, what have you done to me?" he whispered.

And Edie lifted her head and looked up at him, then reached up to brush a lock of hair off his forehead as she smiled and, trusting her instincts, gave him her heart as she had just given him her body.

"I love you, Nick," she told him. Then she eased away and drew herself across his chest to touch her lips to his. "I love you," she told him. "I love you."

He went still. Rigid. His gaze, which moments ago had been fierce with passion, was blank now. Dark and unreadable. Remote. His fingers, which had tangled in her hair and played along her spine, moved away, pulled back.

All that was left was a strained, haunted look in his eyes as he rasped out a single harsh word. "Don't."

CHAPTER NINE

"Don't what?"

Something was different. Wrong.

She could feel it. Could see it in Nick's face. A muscle in his jaw twitched. His teeth seemed clenched, and when he opened his mouth he drew a slow breath before he said evenly, "Don't fall in love with me."

Edie swallowed. Then she smiled and tried desperately to recapture the intimacy of their lovemaking, saying gamely, "Too late. I already have."

She would have rested her head against his chest once more, but he reached out and caught her arms, lifting her away from him, settling her on the bed while he shoved away.

"Nick?" She reached out a hand to him.

But he didn't see it. He was already off the bed with his back turned, reaching for his clothes, his voice still harsh as he muttered, "Damn it."

Damn it? Damn what?

Edie sat up, drawing the sheet around her naked body, suddenly cold as she stared at Nick's back. It was the same back, broad and strong and smooth, that she'd run her fingers over only minutes ago, the same whose spine those fingers had tripped lightly down.

Now it was a wall, keeping her out, his hard, tense muscles almost quivering with emotion. "Nick."

He spun around to face her. "You knew better," he said harshly.

Knew better than to fall in love with him, he meant. She understood what he was accusing her of. But she knew something else with even more certainty.

"I know you," she said with quiet conviction. "You love me, too."

He gave his head a quick, sharp shake. "No."

The flat denial was like a blow. Emotionally it rocked her, but outwardly she refused to flinch. "No? Then what are we doing here?" She waved her hand to encompass not just the room, not just the bed where they had just spent the night in each other's arms, but everything that had happened between them since he'd come to Santa Barbara. "What have we been doing this past month?"

He met her gaze. "Enjoying each other."

Now it was Edie's turn to shake her head. "No. It's more than that."

But Nick folded his arms across his chest. "You're dreaming," he told her. "You're seeing what you want to see."

What she wanted to see—love, commitment, honesty, a future, the two of them together for the rest of their lives—yes, indeed, that's exactly what she was seeing.

"What's wrong with that?" she asked him. When she had given him those words a few minutes ago, warm and languid from their lovemaking, the world had seemed golden, full of promise. Now, in the face of his implacability she felt as if a cloud had crossed the sun.

"It's not going to happen."

"You're saying you don't care?" she said slowly.

"I care." At least he would admit that. "You're a friend. You're a wonderful woman." His words were awkward, but the sentiment was worse. It came out stilted and insincere, stabbing her like a knife.

But she managed a brittle smile. "A good lover?" she suggested with saccharine sweetness. All her earlier euphoria was evaporating now. She felt cold and hurt and scared. Worse, almost, than when she'd learned that Ben had died. Ben couldn't help what had happened.

But Nick—Nick was choosing to reject her love, to deny her and himself.

"A good lover. A great lover," he corrected, not hearing or admitting to hearing her bitterness. He had stepped into his shorts, but he paused and smiled at her now before pulling on his trousers, as if she might forget this nonsense, invite him back to bed and give him an encore.

Not a chance.

Edie got out of bed, too. She felt sick. Her whole body was trembling. She didn't believe what he was saying, but she knew that didn't matter.

What mattered was that *Nick* believed it.

She began dressing quickly, as if putting on clothes would somehow warm her. But of course it wasn't the day that was cold, it was the feeling growing inside her. "I'll be sure to put that on my résumé." She could barely get the words out past the lump in her throat. She struggled into her shirt and began to fumble with the buttons. Damn her fingers, anyway.

Nick's gaze narrowed. "What's that supposed to mean?"

She turned her back to him and stepped into her canvas pants. "Just saying." She tried to toe her sandals out from under the bed. Somehow getting dressed fully was important. It was like putting on armor. Too late, perhaps, but she did what she had to do.

She had her pants zipped up when Nick reached out and caught her by the arm. "Edie."

She tried to pull away, but he held her fast, drew her around so that he looked down into her face. His dear face. His beloved face. His resolutely, implacably closed face.

"You're making too much out of this."

"No."

"Yes," he insisted. "We have a good thing."

"I thought we did," she agreed, her throat aching. "I hoped." Her voice broke.

Damn it! She didn't want to betray how badly this was hurting her. But then, why not? She'd already admitted to loving him.

"You knew that wasn't on. It wasn't what I wanted. Ever," he insisted. "We discussed it."

"What about what I wanted?" she demanded.

He just looked at her. "You're changing the rules."

"Me? You changed them when you came after me!"

He opened his mouth, and for a moment she thought he might deny it. But then he just pressed his lips together in a grim line and shrugged. "It was a good night."

As if he'd done it all because of that. "You came halfway around the world! You took on the restoration of a third-class adobe ranch house when you could have been doing an historically significant Scottish castle."

"I'm going to do the castle. It's where I'm going next."

"When you finish here?"

"Yes."

"When you finish with me!"

Her words made a muscle in his jaw jump. His eyes flashed at the deliberate provocation. Deny it, she begged him silently.

But he didn't. "Yes." The word hissed furiously between his teeth.

She wrenched out of his grasp. "Fine. I'll save you the trouble." She jammed her feet into her sandals, grabbed her phone off the bedside table and clattered down the stairs.

Nick hurtled after her and caught her at the door. "What are you doing?"

"Leaving."

"What? Where are you going? You live here!"

"Yes, well, I don't want to be here right now." And she

grabbed a sweater off the back of a chair and her purse and car keys off the kitchen table.

"Come on," she said to Roy.

"Edie! Stop it. Don't be ridiculous. If someone needs to go, I'll leave."

"Fine. Leave. Go to hell. I don't care." Which was a lie, of course. She wouldn't be close to tears if she didn't care, if she didn't love him with all her heart. She wrenched open the door and clattered down the stairs, Roy following.

Nick came after her in hot pursuit. "Edie! Damn it!"

But she didn't stop. She didn't listen. And she had no intention of standing there listening to Nick tell her that she was being unreasonable. Reason had nothing whatever to do with this. Her response to him had been gut-level since the moment she'd seen him across the dance floor talking to her sister. It had been gut-level when he'd come back, though she'd tried her best to avoid allowing her emotions to control things. For the past month, after learning it had been his idea to come here, not her mother's to bring him, she had dared to believe that he had trusted his emotions as well.

Apparently not. Apparently he was as determined not to care as he'd ever been. So she wasn't staying here. Couldn't. Not now. Not when there was no future for them.

"Edie! For heaven's sake!"

But Edie wasn't listening. She opened the door of her car, let Roy jump in, then climbed in beside him, stuck the key in the ignition and started the engine.

"Don't be an idiot!" He grabbed the door, but not soon enough. She'd hit the power locks an instant before. "Edie!"

But she put the car in gear and took off, refusing to look back, blinking away tears as she went. So much for trusting her instincts.

He let her go.

There was no point in jumping in his car and going after her.

He didn't want her doing something reckless, something foolish. Though it seemed, despite his warning, she already had: she'd fallen in love with him.

There was no point in trying to talk to her, to make her see that wanting too much was asking for trouble, tempting fate. Though God knew, she of all people, having lost a husband, ought to understand about tempting fate.

So be it, he thought as he stood there, staring as the taillights of her car disappeared around the curve in the driveway. But even as he did so, he willed her to slow down, to turn the car around, to come back and wrap her arms around him, to let him wrap his around her, to be grateful for what they had.

It was enough, damn it! She ought to be satisfied with that. He was, he told himself as he punched his fist into the garage retaining wall.

She drove to the beach out by the university, parked her car and began to walk. And walk. It would clear her head, she told herself. It would give her some perspective. It was where she had gone after the debacle with Kyle.

She'd been standing there, staring out at the water, wallowing in mortification, when Ben had jogged by her, stopped and grinned and said, "I know you."

What followed, of course, had changed her life completely.

She wasn't the same person she'd been in those days. At eighteen she had been innocent and idealistic. Kyle's perfidy had wounded her pride and made her feel foolish for having believed they had something when they hadn't.

But at twenty-five she had a great deal more life experience. She knew what was real and what was a pipe dream. She was sure she wasn't wrong believing that she and Nick could have something special. She was sure he loved her just as she loved him.

Nick was the one who was wrong. He didn't believe. He didn't trust.

And she couldn't make him.

Neither could she take back the words she'd spoken. There was no going back, no way of pretending.

She wasn't sorry. She couldn't have lived that lie. She wouldn't live it.

But she couldn't stay here, either. Not if he was going to stay.

She sighed and stared out toward the islands, tried to think what to do, where to go, how to handle the disaster her life was becoming.

Down the beach toward her, a man came jogging. He had dark shaggy hair like Ben. He was lean and slightly knock-kneed like Ben. He came closer. And closer—and ran straight past her without even glancing her way.

Edie smiled a wry self-deprecating smile. There was no Ben to rescue her this time. No Ben could. Not this time. Because this time her love was real, and no amount of serendipity would allow her to deny it.

But that was the thing about serendipity. You couldn't predict it. Never in a million years would she had guessed her mobile phone would ring that moment and Mona would say, "Ruud's broken his leg."

Bangkok was hot and steamy and crowded. Edie was crumpled, exhausted and hollow-eyed, wishing she was numb twenty-four hours later when Mona fell on her neck in gratitude.

"Oh, thank God, you're here!"

Edie stood in the middle of the main room of Mona's beautiful old teak house and let herself be swept into her mother's embrace. She tottered a little under the impact of Mona's enthusiasm, then got her balance as Mona gave her one more squeeze and stepped back to assess her from head to toe.

"Good heavens, you look terrible."

Thank you very much, Edie thought. *Terrible* was actually an improvement on how she felt. She was exhausted physically, shattered emotionally and still unable to get Nick out of her head.

"Surely the flights weren't that bad." Mona was towing her toward one of the rattan sofas and pushing her down.

"No," Edie said. The flights had nothing to do with it.

"Rhiannon?" Mona guessed. "I know she and Andrew have been having a set-to again."

"Have they?" Edie didn't know that. She supposed Rhiannon might have said, but she'd been too busy with Nick to pay much attention.

"Don't cover for them," Mona said firmly. "And I know I have wanted you to make things right in the past, but honestly, Edie, don't worry about them. If they can't solve their own love life problems, it's not your job to do it for them."

Right. Especially since she couldn't even deal with her own.

"And I didn't expect you to drop everything and fly halfway across the world just for Ruud and his leg," Mona added. "Not that I'm sorry you did," she added cheerfully, "because we both know Ruud behaves better for you than for me. And he and Dirk and Grace have missed you terribly. But," Mona added, "I did think you had more pressing things in your own life…" And her perfectly plucked brows lifted in silent query.

Edie knew exactly what they were asking. And she had no intention of answering.

"I was glad to come," she said firmly. "I've missed you—all of you. Where's Ruud? I'm so eager to see them."

And even more eager not to be subjected to more questions. She must have convinced Mona that she really was thrilled to be here because after directing the houseboy to put suitcases in her room, she beckoned to her daughter to follow.

"I didn't tell any of them you were coming," she said. "I wanted them to be surprised."

They were surprised, and as thrilled as Mona had promised they would be. Ruud's face lit up. Dirk flung himself at her. And Grace gave her a hug and said, "I'm sooo glad you're here."

Edie assured them she was glad, too. And, of course, they believed her. Why shouldn't they? They had been the focus of her life since she'd come home after Ben's death. They had no reason to think anything was different now.

And, really, it wasn't different, was it?

Certainly when she'd announced she was leaving, Nick had done nothing to stop her. True, he'd raised his eyebrows. But ultimately he'd just shrugged.

"You do what you have to do," he'd told her.

Short of killing him, which was seriously tempting, she did what she had to do: she left. She moved on.

She knew that if she stayed, she wouldn't be able to do that. She'd be stuck wanting what she couldn't have. And she wasn't going to settle for the affair he was willing to allow her.

No, damn it. It wouldn't be easy, but she was going to forget him.

Forget her!

It should have been a mantra, Nick's mind repeated it so often. He felt sometimes as if the words were emblazoned on the insides of his eyelids. They weren't, of course.

There wasn't room. That was where all the images of Edie resided—the ones that plagued him every time he closed his eyes.

There was Edie in the swimming pool, her dark hair streaming, her eyes alight with mischief. There was Edie in the adobe, prowling, poking, looking wistful, reminiscing. There was Edie tossing a salad, Edie across the dinner table, Edie at the Biltmore, smiling at him over her wineglass, offering him a bite of her pasta. There were visions of Edie romping with Roy, Edie feeding Gerald, Edie standing on the parapet at Mont Chamion, looking out over the fairy lights. There was Edie dancing barefoot. Edie in his arms.

Edie in bed.

So many, many memories of Edie in his bed. In *her* bed. Dear God, he couldn't get them out of his mind.

The memories should have been enough. More than enough. He should have had his fill of her by now, be ready to move on.

But he hadn't. He wasn't.

And though he'd gone to the adobe to work the afternoon she'd left the house, he felt as if she were with him, humming in the other room, just out of sight. He couldn't believe she was getting on an airplane, going to Thailand, for heaven's sake!

It was stupid! Insane!

What they'd had together was amazing, marvelous. Unlike anything he'd ever had before with any woman—except for Amy.

No...not even Amy had been like Edie. *No one* was like Edie. No one made him laugh the way she did. No one was quite as enchanting. No one teased and tempted and at the same time gave so unstintingly of herself.

She had made him happy. And he obviously had made her happy because she claimed to have fallen in love with him.

And yet the stubborn woman threw it all away.

Fine, he told himself angrily. *So be it.*

If he'd got over Amy's death, he could certainly get over Edie walking out. He didn't need her. He didn't want her. Permanence, commitment—*love!*—was the last thing he wanted!

So he'd forget her. He'd finish up the adobe because it was his job—and he'd never mix business and pleasure again.

Never.

"Miss? There is a gentleman..." Malee, the housekeeper, opened the door a crack to the room Edie was using for an office. She smiled apologetically when Edie looked up, startled.

"A gentleman?" Edie felt the bottom drop out of her stomach at the same time hope went winging heavenward. She shut her eyes. Thank God. "Show him in," she said, wiping damp palms on the sides of her linen trousers as she stood up and tried to compose herself.

It had been a week. She'd almost given up hope. She took a deep breath as Malée pushed the door open wider and stepped back.

Kyle Robbins walked into the room. "Edie!" The trademark gorgeous Robbins grin lit his face.

Edie felt the light go out of hers. "Kyle," she said dully. Her stomach felt like lead.

He raised his brows as he read her body language. "Good to see you, too," he said with obvious irony.

"I—wasn't expecting you." Edie hoped she didn't come down too hard on the "you" part of that sentence. "What are you doing here?" she demanded. "If Mona put you up to this—"

"Mona invited me," he said, "to go over a script with her. We're doing a film together next month. You know that," he reminded her. "You set up this meeting." Which, now that Edie thought about it, was the absolute truth.

Mona habitually asked to spend a week or so going over a script with the other actors she'd be working with. Kyle was one of those actors. And now that he mentioned it, Edie did vaguely remember setting up this meeting.

But she'd done it when her every thought had been revolving around Nick. And it was testimony to how little Kyle mattered anymore that the emails she'd exchanged with him had barely even registered on her radar.

"I forgot," she said, shrugging lamely.

Kyle grimaced wryly. "Which pretty much shows me where I stand."

"Yes," Edie said frankly.

He nodded. "I'm sorry. Many years too late. I was an idiot. I handled things badly."

"You were unfaithful," Edie corrected.

He winced, but then he nodded. "Like I said, I was a fool. But—" he sighed "—Jake is the one thing about my marriage I don't regret."

And he turned and through the doorway, Edie could see that Kyle hadn't come alone. Out in the other room a young boy sat on the sofa. The baby Serena had been expecting, the reason Kyle had broken off his relationship with Edie.

"If I'd known you were here, I would never have—"

But Edie shook her head. "I'd like to meet him," she said quite honestly.

Kyle's eyes lit up. "He's a great kid. You'll love him. Maybe you and I—"

"No," Edie said.

But she would like to meet Jake. And she imagined Jake would like to meet the twins. If he was going to be around for a week or so, they could have a good time—and she could keep even busier.

She needed to stay busy—because Nick wasn't coming after her. She'd hoped. But he'd had a week. If it were going to happen, it would have happened by now.

She needed to face facts, needed to face the truth.

She might love Nick Savas fervently and foolishly, but however much she might wish it was otherwise, Nick wasn't willing—or wasn't able—to return her love.

She wasn't coming back.

He'd thought she would. Even though he'd told himself to forget her, that she didn't matter, that he was better off without her, deep down somewhere inside him, Nick couldn't quite manage to convince himself.

So he did the next best thing. He told himself she'd realize she was wrong, that she was throwing away something good—and she'd come back.

He would be gracious about it. He wouldn't say, "I told you so," even if he had. He wouldn't point out how foolish she'd been to run or how much time she'd wasted that they could have been spending together.

He'd just smile and hold out his arms to her. He'd catch her up in an embrace and carry her off to bed and show her what she'd been missing.

Every time he thought about doing that, he smiled.

It was pretty much the only time he smiled all day. He spent almost every waking hour at the adobe working his tail off. He might as well. He had nothing else to do with his waking hours. And the hours he was supposed to be sleeping—well, he wasn't doing much of that. He might as well have been working then, too.

When she came back, he'd show her how much he'd accomplished. She'd love it. She'd smile and tell him about growing up there. She'd make him see it in his mind's eye. But then every day that she didn't come back, his hopes faded a little bit more.

And then a week after she left, he was dragging himself back, grim and exhausted, to Mona's house one evening, when Roy ran ahead, barking.

Nick came around the corner of the garage and saw a strange car in the driveway. The trunk lid was up. The front door was open.

He stopped and stared. Hope soared.

Then he started to grin, and scrubbed eagerly at his filthy face with the T-shirt slung round his neck. He began to sprint toward the door—and skidded to a halt as a woman came out of it.

"Rhiannon?"

It was, with Roy bouncing eagerly around her. Edie's sister paid Roy no attention at all. She was staring at Nick, equally stunned.

"Where's Edie?" she demanded.

"In Thailand."

Rhiannon frowned. "In Thailand? Why? Who are you?"

She didn't *know?* He guessed he shouldn't be surprised. "Nick Savas. We met at my cousin's wedding. What are you doing here?"

Whatever answer he might have thought he was expecting, he wasn't expecting the one he got. She burst into tears.

"I need Edie!" Great noisy sobs erupted and her face grew blotchy and red. It seemed far too theatrical to be real, but a moment's reflection told him that she couldn't possibly be doing this on purpose. These sorts of sobs made her far too ugly.

"For God's sake, Rhiannon," he said, caught halfway between wanting to pat her on the back and wanting to run in the other direction. "Stop that! What's wrong?"

She gulped, started to speak. Then started crying again and he had to wait for her to stop to get an answer at last. "Andrew's b-broken our en-g-gagement!" And, of course, the tears started up again.

Nick shifted from one foot to the other. He debated offering her his filthy T-shirt to mop up her face, then decided against it. "I'm sure he didn't mean it," he said awkwardly, not sure at all.

"H-he did!" Rhiannon dug in the pockets of her jeans and came up with a handkerchief that looked as if it had seen her through earlier bouts of tears. "And—and I deserve it. It's all… all my f-fault!"

Now that Nick could believe.

"I was trying to make him jealous. He spends so much time swimming! Matt doesn't mean anything!"

Uh-oh.

"He's just a f-friend. But Andrew got the wrong idea. Edie s-says I don't think Andrew has feelings."

He could believe that, too. "Go inside," he ordered her. "I'll bring in your cases, then make you a cup of tea."

Rhiannon managed a watery smile. "A cup of tea?"

He shrugged, feeling stupid and awkward.

But she nodded and sniffed. "Tea would b-be good. Edie makes me tea. You're like Edie."

He wasn't, God knew. On the other hand, it might be the biggest compliment he'd ever received.

He brought in her cases, put on the kettle, then went upstairs, scrubbed his face and pulled a clean shirt over his head. He wished she'd go away, and yet at the same time, he was glad she was here. She was a link to her sister, even if she obviously hadn't spoken to Edie in days.

When he came back downstairs, Rhiannon was coming out of the powder room. She'd washed her face, too, but it was still blotchy and her eyes were bloodshot.

"I don't know what to do." She trailed after him into the kitchen, like a lost soul. "What should I do?"

Nick made tea and thrust the mug into her hand. "Drink this."

She took a sip. Then, clutching the mug as if it were a life preserver, Rhiannon carried it to the sofa and curled up in one corner. "Edie would know what to do." She sobbed into her tea mug, then lifted her gaze and fixed it on Nick. "What should I do?"

As if he were some love-and-marriage guru. As if he were Edie. What would Edie do?

He asked, "Where is Andrew?"

"Here."

Nick looked around, wondering if somehow he hadn't noticed Andrew in the room. "Where's here?"

"At home. His parents live about a mile from here. He's with th-them." She was sobbing again. "He won't talk to me."

"Have you tried?"

"N-no."

"Well, then—"

"He says h-he's done. That he's getting a new girlfriend! He says he hates me."

That was the first thing that sounded promising. "He doesn't," Nick said firmly. "Go talk to him."

"But—"

"Listen." Nick sat down beside her on the couch and leaned toward her, absolutely earnest. "If Andrew says he hates you, he's trying not to love you. He's not there yet."

Rhiannon looked at him, eyes wide. She sniffed. Twice. "Are you s-sure?"

Was he? What the hell did he know about love?

A lot, came the wholly unexpected answer. He'd been in love once. He was in love now—with Edie.

The recognition hit him like a fist in the gut.

"But what if he has a new girlfriend?" Rhiannon was demanding.

It didn't matter. Just like it hadn't mattered that Derek WhatsHisName had tried to muscle into Edie's life. "What if he does?" Nick challenged her. "Are you just going to sit back and let her have him?"

"I—" She stopped and looked at him helplessly.

"You can," Nick said, "if he doesn't matter to you. Or if you can pretend he doesn't matter." He let the words sink in. "Or—" his eyes bored into hers "—you can take a risk."

Take a risk. Take a risk. Take a risk. The words pounded inside his head.

Rhiannon didn't answer. She stared at him. Then she stared into the mug of tea. Nick didn't care what she did. The words were beating a tattoo in his brain.

Then Rhiannon lifted her gaze and met his. "I'm going to take the risk."

Her words dropped like stones in a quiet pool. Nick could almost see the ripples. Certainly he could feel them.

She didn't finish her tea. She put the mug on the counter, ran a brush through her hair, dabbed her cheeks dry again, but at the last minute grabbed a tissue box to take with her.

"Just in case" she told Nick who was still sitting on the couch, her words—a reply to his own challenge—still echoing in his head.

She paused beside him, then bent to kiss his cheek. "Thank you," she said. "I hope you're right."

Nick watched her go. As soon as she was out the door, he picked up his phone and called the airline, hoping to God that he was right, too.

CHAPTER TEN

THE problem with running away when you were an adult was that, eventually, you had to go home.

Edie knew that. She accepted it. She'd just hoped she would have done a better job of putting Nick behind her before she did so.

God knew she'd tried. She'd thrown herself with a vengeance into life in Thailand. Besides doing her regular work for Mona, she'd spent vast amounts of time with the twins and Grace. And because he was there, and he really didn't matter to her now, she even found herself going out with Kyle and his son, Jake.

But however much time she spent with them all, it wasn't enough.

No matter where she was, no matter what she was doing, Nick was always with her.

She wouldn't be able to move on until she'd gone home and faced him—or at least faced the renovation of the adobe he'd left behind. That might not work, either. But since Mona's film was finished and they were all leaving the country, it was the only hope she had.

"You don't have to go home," Kyle told her when she brought him his boarding passes that afternoon. He and Jake were going to the Caribbean for a couple of weeks before Kyle started work with Mona on the new film. Now he was sitting in Mona's garden watching Jake roughhouse with Dirk. But after tucking the boarding passes into his pocket, he turned to her with a brilliant smile and said, "Tear yours up. Come with us."

Edie shook her head. "Thanks, but I can't."

"You're not happy," Kyle pointed out. That had been obvious to everyone, though Edie had done her best to pretend.

Now she shrugged. "So I should bring my unhappiness to you?" She laughed a little ruefully. "Thanks, but I don't think so."

"I could make you happy," Kyle said with his customary confidence. But then his grin faded a little and he said, "I could try, Edie."

"Kyle—"

"I know you said forget it. But we were good together once— until I screwed it up. I was a fool." He shook his head. "I'll always regret that."

"But you don't regret Jake."

And he turned his gaze to watch his son playing with the twins. For a long moment he watched, and then he turned back to her. "No," he said quietly. "I don't regret that."

They both stood silently then, and Edie wondered if she was being a fool, too, throwing away a chance at some sort of happiness just because it wasn't with the man she really wanted?

But there was only one answer to that.

"Thank you," she said, looking up into his eyes, smiling and shaking her head. "But I can't. I will always be your friend, but I don't love you."

Kyle's expression was rueful. "Nothing more than I deserve," he allowed. "Still, if you change your mind, you'll know where to find me." Then he dipped his head and kissed her on the lips.

"What in the hell are you kissing him for?"

Edie spun around. *Nick?*

Yes, Nick! Stone-faced and furious, Nick was standing in the living room glaring at her. Behind him by the open front door, a nervous Malee was wringing her hands.

Edie stared, stunned, her mind reeling. What was he doing

here? Her pulses started to pound. More to the point, why did he care who she kissed? He didn't want her—except in his bed.

Now she bristled. "I'll kiss whoever I want!" She drew herself up and glared right back at him. "And for that matter, what the hell are you doing here?"

His jaw worked. He was still holding a duffel bag, which he dumped on the floor. "I need to talk to you." His gaze was glittering, his chest heaving.

"About what?" Edie asked, afraid to hope. She'd already done that. Couldn't do it again.

"You don't have to talk to him," Kyle said quietly.

"She damned well does," Nick bit out.

"You don't," Kyle insisted, stepping between her and Nick. She thought Nick might pick him up and throw him into the pond.

"Do you want to talk to him?" Kyle asked her. "Or should I beat him to a pulp?"

"Like to see you try," Nick ground out.

Kyle didn't back down. Nick took a step forward. Malee, the twins and Jake all sucked in a collective breath.

"Let him talk," Edie said unsteadily. "What's so important that you came halfway around the world?"

His eyes were fixed on her, still glittering. "Rhiannon needed you," he told her. "You weren't there."

His words crushed any hope she had left. She felt numb. "And you came all the way to Thailand to tell me that?" It didn't make any sense.

Nick shook his head. "No, but it got me here."

"I don't understand." Had something happened to her sister? There had been messages from Rhiannon. Lots of them. But Edie had taken a page out of Mona's book. She'd made up her mind to stop trying to fix Rhiannon's love life. Now, all of a sudden Edie felt dread.

"What happened to Rhiannon?" she demanded.

"I'll tell you," Nick answered evenly, "but I'd prefer it without an audience."

"You don't have to listen to him, Edie," Kyle reminded her.

Nick opened his mouth, but Edie cut him off. "It's all right. Come on," she said to Nick. "We'll go in the office."

She led the way, aware of him right behind her. But she didn't look back until he'd shut the door behind them.

Then she turned and demanded, "Tell me! What about Rhiannon? What's happened?"

Nick grinned faintly. "She's fine. All patched up with Andrew. Married to him, as a matter of fact."

Edie's legs felt suddenly like jelly. "*What?!*"

Nick shrugged. "I wasn't quite expecting that, either. But she came home three days ago. No, maybe four—what day is it?"

"Friday," Edie said absently. "Tell me." She had to be hearing things.

"Right." He dragged a hand through his hair. He looked terrible. Sleepless, pale, with dark circles under his eyes, hair rumpled and at least a couple of days stubble on his jaw. And beautiful, too. She wanted to reach out to him, to touch him. She didn't dare. So she balled her fingers into fists.

"She came looking for you," Nick said. "Crying. The world had ended. Andrew was finished with her. It was all her fault. She loved him so." Nick looked harassed at the memory.

Edie nodded. Yes, that sounded pretty much like Rhiannon.

"Wanted to know what she should do," Nick went on. "I mean, how the hell should I know?" Now he looked beyond harassed. He began pacing around the small office, rubbing his hand through his hair, kneading the muscles at the back of his neck.

"You who don't do relationships, you mean?"

He shot her a glance and then hunched his shoulders. "Pretty much. So I thought, what would you do?"

"And what would I do?" Edie asked curiously.

He shrugged. "I made her a cup of tea."

Edie swallowed a smile. She didn't feel like smiling. She felt like crying. "I'm sure that helped," she said gravely, past the lump in her throat.

"It did," Nick said shortly. "And then I told her to go talk to him. Told her he still loved her."

"How would you know a thing like that?"

"Because, damn it, she said he'd told her he wasn't going to. Like it was a choice!"

"I thought it was a choice," Edie reminded him quietly.

"That's rubbish," Nick said flatly. "You can't stop it. It's destiny." He was looking square at her. "Like I love you."

The world stopped. Sound stopped. Well, maybe not sound. Edie could hear the twins and Jake yelling in the garden. But all the rest of the sounds in the world.

And her heart. Her heart stopped, too.

She stared at him. Mute. Disbelieving.

"I love you," Nick repeated, his voice ragged. He looked miserable.

"And that's what you came to tell me?" Edie ventured, unsure, though her heart was singing, whether this was a good thing or not. Nick certainly didn't look as if he were thrilled by the discovery.

He looked as uncertain as she felt. And then he demanded, voice cracking, "Whatever happened to 'I love you, too'?"

And then Edie understood. She saw his pain for what it was— fear. But he had vanquished it. He had said the words. He'd believed them!

And that was what mattered. She flew to him then, and threw her arms around him. "I love you, too!" And she kissed his rough chin, his stubbled jaw, his warm, hungry mouth.

Nick caught her to him, kissing her, wrapping her in an embrace so tight she could barely breathe. It didn't matter. What breath she had was for him. She kissed him back, hungry for him, desperate for him. She wanted him here and now, but there was one office chair in this room—and one small desk.

He looked around at the same time she did, saw what she saw and came to the same conclusion, saying ruefully, "Bad planning."

She laughed unsteadily. "Later," she promised. Then, "There will be later, won't there?"

"Please, God," Nick said fervently.

"There will," Edie vowed. "There will," she said again, knowing he needed to hear it. "It won't be like Amy."

"You don't know that," Nick said roughly.

"You're right, of course. I don't. I don't know what happened."

"She had an aneurysm," Nick said. "No one knew she had anything wrong. Then, two days before the wedding, she just—" He stopped, couldn't go on.

Edie kissed him again, then rested her cheek against his. "I'm sorry. So very sorry."

"So am I. It was my fault."

"Aneurysms aren't anyone's fault," Edie protested.

"Not that. Putting off the wedding. She didn't care about the house being done. I shouldn't have made her wait."

"You can't second guess that," Edie told him.

"I know. And yet—" he shook his head wearily "—I couldn't help it. I wanted to die, too. I never wanted to go through it again. I chose not to." He raised his head and met her gaze now. "At least I tried to."

"I'm glad it doesn't work like that," Edie said softly. She still had his fingers wrapped in hers. They lay against his chest, and beneath them she could feel the steady solid beat of his heart.

"I am, too." Nick turned his head and his lips touched her forehead. He kissed her. He kissed her hair. "Will you marry me?"

As much as she wanted to hear the words, when she did, they were unexpected. "Is that what you want?" she asked, needing to be sure.

Nick nodded. "It is." A corner of his mouth quirked. "I asked Rhiannon if she was going to fight for Andrew, if she dared to take the risk. She did. And I knew that if she had enough guts to go after what she wanted, I should damned well take the risk for you." He bent his head and touched his lips to hers. "I love you, Edie."

And Edie believed then. Trusted. And put her heart in his keeping. "I love you, too. And yes, please, I'll marry you."

His wedding day scared the hell out of him.

Not that Nick let on.

He figured Edie knew. She seemed to know what he was thinking even before he thought it. But everyone else was focusing on the bride. So was he. He wasn't superstitious. He didn't think lightning struck in the same place twice. But he couldn't stop worrying. He didn't want to lose her.

If Amy had been his first love, Edie was his forever love. She was his heart and his soul. She gave the meaning to every breath he took.

And as he waited for her to come down the stairs of her mother's house and walk out onto the *ramada* in her bridal gown to marry him, he knew that his heart was hammering, his collar was strangling him, his fingers shook.

Next to him, his cousin Yiannis, the best man, murmured, "You're not going to faint, are you?"

And the terrible thing was, Nick couldn't promise that he wouldn't. He couldn't say anything at all. He could only wait.

And then, there she was—his beautiful dark-haired bride, his Edie—coming to meet him, her eyes alight with joy, her smile just for him.

He breathed again.

"Thank God," Yiannis murmured.

"Have you got the ring?" Nick asked under his breath.

"Ring?" Yiannis looked blank. Then at Nick's look of pure terror, he grinned. "I've got it right here." He patted his pocket. "No getting out of it now."

"I don't want to," Nick said as Edie reached him and he took her hand in his. "Let's do this."

They did it.

Short, sweet. An absolutely perfect wedding with only family and close friends around, followed by a reception for Rhiannon and Andrew as well as for them. It had been going on for hours.

But Nick and Edie weren't there.

They were going on their honeymoon.

"Where are we going for our honeymoon?" she asked. "Why won't you tell me?"

"You'll see soon enough," he said.

"Will I like it?"

"I hope so."

They were in her apartment getting ready to leave. They could hear the music and the dancing and the celebration across the driveway in the house. Rhiannon and Andrew were enjoying it immensely. Nick was glad they had been there. He was ready to move on.

"I don't even know what to bring," she said plaintively. "I don't know what to wear."

"I've packed for you. And what you've got on is fine for now," he told her. She'd changed out of her wedding dress into a pair of shorts and a T-shirt just to relax.

"This?" She looked askance.

"Perfect," he told her. He grabbed the bag he'd packed in one hand and took hers in the other. "Come on."

He took her down the stairs, but when she would have gone toward the car in the garage, he turned the other way, toward the trees.

Suddenly Edie stopped, and Nick knew she understood. "Nick?" She had a stranglehold on his hand and was looking at him, her eyes wide, wondering.

He gave her a gentle tug. "Come on."

She hadn't been to the adobe since they'd come back from

Thailand. She hadn't had much time. They'd arranged the wedding in less than a week. And the few times she had suggested going to check out his progress, he'd found reasons to put it off.

Now he felt a flicker of the old familiar fear as he took her hand and led her up the hill and down the other side to where the old adobe waited.

A softly glowing porch light welcomed them in the waning twilight. It looked good. The front steps were solid, the porch wide, with low-slung wood and leather Spanish style chairs for sitting outside on a warm afternoon.

Edie looked at it, her lips parted in amazement. The outside walls had all been finished with lime plaster. All the *vigas* and corbels had been repaired or replaced and the roof was whole again. Lights shone from within through the deep-set windows.

"It's beautiful," she murmured. "It's far more beautiful than I remembered." Now she grabbed his hand and, instead of going up the steps to the porch, she dragged him around the back to beam at the porch now painted and finished. She hugged him hard, her eyes shining. "It's perfect." Then she went up on the porch and peered through the windows.

"Furniture?" She turned back to look at him.

"Some. You didn't think we were going to sleep on the floor, did you?"

"I didn't think we were going to spend our honeymoon here!"

"Are you sorry?" He'd thought it would be perfect, but now he wondered if perhaps he'd been mistaken.

But Edie was smiling. "Not at all. It's the best place." She ran her hand down one of the support beams. "It's how I knew you loved me."

He stared at her. "What?"

"You would never have suggested renovating a third-rate run-down old building if you didn't," she told him cheerfully. "Would you?"

He thought about it, logically, analytically, sensibly—and knew that she was right. "I guess I wouldn't."

Now it was his turn to take her by the hand and lead her around to the front of the house, to take her up the steps onto the wide front porch. There he stopped and took down the envelope that had been tacked to the door. He handed it to Edie. "It's for you."

Edie's fingers trembled as she took it. Slowly she fumbled it open. Then she bent her head and read it—at first silently, then aloud.

"My darling daughter," she began, her voice wavering. "There was always love in this house when your dad and I lived here. I wish you and Nick a lifetime of the same sort of love. The house is yours. I know you and Nick will make it a wonderful home. I hope the memories you already have and the memories you make are as wonderful as you are. I love you, Mom."

Tears slid down her cheeks. Sniffling, Edie tried to wipe them away.

"Here," Nick said gently, and he bent his head and kissed them away one by one.

"Mom," Edie said, with a quiet laugh. "Mom." She hadn't called her mother that in years. But it was right. Everything was right.

"Not Mona," Nick agreed.

"Just wait until there's someone to call her Grandma," Edie said with sudden glee.

Nick laughed, too. "I can't wait. I love you." And he swept her up into his arms, kicked open the door and carried her over the threshold into the home of her past and of their future. "In fact, Mrs. Savas, I think we should get started on that someone right now."

* * * * *

CLASSIC

Quintessential, modern love stories
that are romance at its finest.

You can find more information on upcoming Harlequin® titles,
free excerpts and more at www.HarlequinInsideRomance.com.

HPECNM1111

REQUEST YOUR
FREE BOOKS!

2 FREE NOVELS PLUS
2 FREE GIFTS!

YES! Please send me 2 FREE Harlequin Presents® novels and my 2 FREE gifts (gifts are worth about $10). After receiving them, if I don't wish to receive any more books, I can return the shipping statement marked "cancel." If I don't cancel, I will receive 6 brand-new novels every month and be billed just $4.30 per book in the U.S. or $4.99 per book in Canada. That's a saving of at least 14% off the cover price! It's quite a bargain! Shipping and handling is just 50¢ per book in the U.S. and 75¢ per book in Canada.* I understand that accepting the 2 free books and gifts places me under no obligation to buy anything. I can always return a shipment and cancel at any time. Even if I never buy another book, the two free books and gifts are mine to keep forever.

106/306 HDN FERQ

Name _____ (PLEASE PRINT)

Address _____ Apt. #

City _____ State/Prov. _____ Zip/Postal Code

Signature (if under 18, a parent or guardian must sign)

Mail to the **Reader Service**:
IN U.S.A.: P.O. Box 1867, Buffalo, NY 14240-1867
IN CANADA: P.O. Box 609, Fort Erie, Ontario L2A 5X3

Not valid for current subscribers to Harlequin Presents books.

**Are you a current subscriber to Harlequin Presents books
and want to receive the larger-print edition?
Call 1-800-873-8635 or visit www.ReaderService.com.**

* Terms and prices subject to change without notice. Prices do not include applicable taxes. Sales tax applicable in N.Y. Canadian residents will be charged applicable taxes. Offer not valid in Quebec. This offer is limited to one order per household. All orders subject to credit approval. Credit or debit balances in a customer's account(s) may be offset by any other outstanding balance owed by or to the customer. Please allow 4 to 6 weeks for delivery. Offer available while quantities last.

*Lucy Flemming and Ross Mitchell shared a magical,
sexy Christmas weekend together six years ago.
This Christmas, history may repeat itself when they find
themselves stranded in a major snowstorm...
and alone at last.*

*Read on for a sneak peek from
IT HAPPENED ONE CHRISTMAS
by Leslie Kelly.*

Available December 2011, only from Harlequin® Blaze™.

EYEING THE GRAY, THICK SKY through the expansive wall of
windows, Lucy began to pack up her photography gear.
The Christmas party was winding down, only a dozen or so
people remaining on this floor, which had been transformed
from cubicles and meeting rooms to a holiday funland. She
smiled at those nearest to her, then, seeing the glances at her
silly elf hat, she reached up to tug it off her head.

Before she could do it, however, she heard a voice. A
deep, male voice—smooth and sexy, and so not Santa's.

"I appreciate you filling in on such short notice. I've
heard you do a terrific job."

Lucy didn't turn around, letting her brain process what
she was hearing. Her whole body had stiffened, the hairs on
the back of her neck standing up, her skin tightening into
tiny goose bumps. Because that voice sounded so familiar.
Impossibly familiar.

It can't be.

"It sounds like the kids had a great time."

Unable to stop herself, Lucy began to turn around,
wondering if her ears—and all her other senses—were
deceiving her. After all, six years was a long time, the mind

could play tricks. What were the odds that she'd bump into *him*, here? And today of all days. December 23.

Six years exactly. Was that really possible?

One look—and the accompanying frantic thudding of her heart—and she knew her ears and brain were working just fine. Because it was *him*.

"Oh, my God," he whispered, shocked, frozen, staring as thoroughly as she was. "Lucy?"

She nodded slowly, not taking her eyes off him, wondering why the years had made him even more attractive than ever. It didn't seem fair. Not when she'd spent the past six years thinking he must have started losing that thick, golden-brown hair, or added a spare tire to that trim, muscular form.

No.

The man was gorgeous. Truly, without-a-doubt, mouth-wateringly handsome, every bit as hot as he'd been the first time she'd laid eyes on him. She'd been twenty-two, he one year older.

They'd shared an amazing holiday season.

And had never seen one another again.

Until now.

Find out what happens in
IT HAPPENED ONE CHRISTMAS
by Leslie Kelly.
Available December 2011, only from Harlequin® Blaze™

Discover two tales of romance
under the mistletoe in one incredible volume from

USA TODAY **Bestselling Author**

Penny Jordan

This Christmas, two women
will take risks for the men
they love and turn business
into pleasure.

MISTLETOE BRIDES

Available November 22, 2011.

www.Harlequin.com

HSC68839